ng House

Piotr Paziński

THE BOARDING HOUSE

Translated from the Polish by Tusia Dabrowska

DALKEY ARCHIVE PRESS

Originally published in Polish by Nisza Publishing House (Poland) as *Pensjonat* in 2009.

Copyright © by Piotr Pazinski, 2009.

Translation copyright © by Tusia Dabrowska, 2018.

Introduction copyright © by Tusia Dabrowska, 2018.

First Dalkey Archive edition, 2018.

Library of Congress Cataloging-in-Publication Data

Names: Paziânski, Piotr, author. | Dabrowska, Tusia, translator.

Title: The boarding house / Piotr Pazinski ; translated by Tusia Dabrowska.

Other titles: Pensjonat. English

Description: First Dalkey Archive edition. | Victoria, TX : Dalkey Archive Press, 2018.

Identifiers: LCCN 2018026041 | ISBN 9781628972726 (pbk. : acid-free paper)

Classification: LCC PG7216.A98 P4613 2018 | DDC 891.8/538--dc23

LC record available at https://lccn.loc.gov/2018026041

Co-funded by the Creative Europe Programme of the European Union

www.dalkeyarchive.com
McLean, IL / Dublin

The European Commission support for the production of this publication does not constitute an endorsement of the contents which reflects the views only of the author, and the commission cannot be held responsible for any use which may be made of the information contained therein.

Printed on permanent/durable acid-free paper

Translator's Note

This is the Borscht Belt of Poland, Piotr explained on our trip to the Środborowianka boarding house in the summer of 2011. Like the narrator in his novel, we caught an early morning train to Otwock, a sleepy town about thirty minutes from Warsaw. I thought I recognized the Świdermajer houses and the pine forest so evocatively described in the book. Our day at the boarding house included dancing with a nonagenarian who, with a pre-World War II elegance, moving randomly from Polish to Yiddish and back, asked me to marry him. An octogenarian shared with us his memoir recently published in English (maybe Hollywood would bite), while another one showed up in his military uniform with a stack of pictures. The women sitting in the beach chairs on the terrace quietly nodded—they have heard it all many times. This strange band of summer vacationers—a rapidly disappearing generation of Holocaust survivors—is at the heart of *The Boarding House*. The novel is a record of a community whose story needs to be protected from historical erasure.

Although the main plot of the book takes place in the aughts, the narrator often returns in his memories to the 1970s, a period sometimes described as "a forgotten decade" of the Polish Jewry. While the government-sponsored anti-Semitic campaign of the fifties and sixties further decimated an already fragile and deeply traumatized community, its remnants continued to exist. For example, TSKZ, or the Cultural Association of Jews in Poland, had a number of "clubs." The *Folks Sztyme* weekly, ŻIH (the Jewish Historical Institute), and the Jewish Theater in Warsaw, among others, kept operating. However, in the now-dominant narratives of the so-called Jewish revival in Poland that took place after the Transformation of 1989, roughly twenty years later, these islands of predominantly secular Jewish life organized and run by the Holocaust generation are often overlooked.

Pazinski's book (not entirely without its predecessors) amends the record. Although *The Boarding House* is classified as fiction, I find this categorization reductive. Even magical elements are weaved into the story in ways that echo the rich literary history of the region's Jewish magical realism. Importantly, the physical place, its mood and its summer visitors, are captured with precision, honesty, respect, and love. The characters in this novel are hardly figments of a writer's imagination. Their stories and their voices ring true to those of us who are familiar with this community. I am convinced that the book is not considered a piece of creative non-fiction for the simple reason that the term itself is not prevalent in Polish literature.

The Boarding House is an exquisite attempt at constructing a folk tale about a community that had lived through an unspeakable trauma, was denied the right to heal (if such healing is even possible), and yet survived in all of its complex, contorted ways. It's a story of loneliness and homesickness that I believe can resonate not just with those who have Jewish Eastern European roots, but all those who come from or have empathy for communities that were traumatized.

It is an important book, and this is why I agreed to translate it. The decision wasn't easy, and the task was harder still. One cold, gray afternoon, a friend called as I was getting on a tram. The *Forward* needs a short section, a few pages. Would I do it? I agreed because Piotr is a good friend, because it seemed like a small favor. But the translation process was harrowing. Apparently, that's not unusual. As Piotr—himself a recognized translator into Polish—says, a translator may pine to translate a book's entire cultural ecosystem, but her task is limited to a single work.

Sometimes a single word can be a challenge. For example, in Polish, a verb's form implies the subject of a sentence; thus it's often natural to skip subjects. This feature of the Polish language invites a poetic quality and ambiguity that cannot always be preserved in English. Even the loss of some awkwardness in the original can be painful to the translator. In *The Boarding House*, when subjects or pronouns are introduced in consecutive sentences—even if technically correct—to a Polish ear, they hint at a fossilized foreign (in this case Yiddish) grammar, as when old Mr. Rubin, dreaming about a young Polish waitress, says: "[W] hat am I doing? I'm just looking. Who said that it's forbidden? I'm still alive!" But in English his repeated use of "I" doesn't register as odd. On the other hand, formal address of elders may sound tiresome to an American ear, but when Ms. Tecia and the Director quarrel, they remain formal. Even when she calls him "a donkey," Ms. Tecia makes sure to address the Director as "sir." And so on.

To translate is to venture to grasp the rhythm, meaning, and nuance of a text, knowing that there will be instances where what lies between words will resist and evade capture. It's to honor an idiosyncrasy of a world depicted by someone else, while making sure that it's not only intelligible but also enticing to a reader in a different world.

And it is my hope that the pages that follow will entice you.

Tusia Dabrowska
May, 2018

Acknowledgments

I WOULD LIKE to begin by expressing my gratitude to Piotr Pazinski for selecting me to translate his book. It took many years of gentle nudging from Piotr, and if it had not been not for his unwavering trust and confidence in me, I would not have found the courage to work on this translation.

However, this project would also not have been possible without the support and help of a number of people.

I would like to acknowledge Jim Lucey, a friend, an outstanding educator, and a patient first reader, whom I recruited to jump (sink?) into this translation process with me.

Note that Piotr reviewed, and provided where necessary, English transliteration of Hebrew and Yiddish. He also added footnotes to the English-language edition.

Den Petrovsky originally suggested I should translate a section of *The Boarding House* that appeared in the *Forward*. I should like to thank him and the media outlet for this opportunity, as well as the *Vassar Review* for publishing a different chapter.

Finally, I'm thankful to the Edward J. Thompson Foundation for the Arts for their generous support, and the Dalkey Archive Press, especially Jake Snyder and John O'Brien, for publishing this book.

1

IN THE BEGINNING, there were train tracks. In the greenery, between heaven and earth. With stations, like beads on a string, placed so close together that even before the train managed to accelerate, it had to slow down in preparation for the following stop. Platforms made of concrete, narrow and shaky, equipped with ladders and steep steps, grew straight out of sand, as though built on dunes. The stations' pavilions resembled old-fashioned kiosks: elongated, bent awnings, and azure letters on both ends, which appeared to float on air.

I've always enjoyed peering at them, beginning with the first station outside the strict limits of the city, when the crowded urban architecture quickly thins out and the world expands to an uncanny size.

Luckily, the tracks remained as I'd left them. They run straight ahead, in a decisive gesture, to melt with the horizon, from here barely visible, hidden behind nature, or, to the contrary—to disappear in a hidden tunnel hollowed out in the sky and then begin running again on the other side, in a completely different and unknown world.

A road wound along the tracks. It was sandy, meandering among heathers, then paved, normal, suburban. Behind the window flickered a land of car-repair shops, snack bars, and motley signs sprayed on snippets of brass. Poorly plastered, cube-shaped houses made of air bricks and roadside fortresses triumphed over wooden architecture. They crouched, spreading comfortably and widely, convinced of their own success, unencumbered by age. A few hovels remained here, perched above the tracks, apologizing for their existence. They held tightly to the grass, yet the grass could not prevent their inevitable decline. Here and there, a lonely pigeon coop stuck out. Large gray birds crowded tightly together on steep awnings, their wings touched and jostled, even though there was plenty of room—room for all, to dot with droppings. Flustered by the roar of the train cars, they rose in flight, made a few nervous rounds above the maze of overhead traction power lines, only to return to their old tasks as the train disappeared on the horizon.

The train was slowing down in the wilderness of cross tracks, passing a sad loading ramp covered by shrubs and rolling, solemnly, into the final station. It must have been around noon, maybe a little later. Nothing else could be gathered from the train schedule. The hands of the station's clock failed to move, and I was not about to wait until they began to rotate, catching up on the lost moments. The crowd flew by in a hurry, dragging heavy luggage, their presence not bothering anyone any longer than necessary.

From there on, I have to walk by foot. It's close by, and I should have no problem finding my way. In this area, decay was less prevalent. It seemed the process of disintegration had slowed its tempo, showing a little mercy to its subjects. In fact, everything has remained the same here, against all rules, rhyme or reason. The sun was still up high above the singular woolly clouds. A web of fall tones loomed over the contours of houses, changing the solid shapes into artistic visions hung in the air, vibrating with light.

There was only one train track because the other one had been dismantled something like a hundred years ago or more. The Vistula River train line. That's what we'd called it at home. Not the Otwock line, but the Vistula River train line. Or, simply, "the line." I don't know why. A name I've heard since forever. Like "Nalewki," or "Plac Krasińskich," "Gęsia 18," and "Świętojerska 13," where at the intersection with Nowiniarska our house was. That is, our house from before the war; however,

Świętojerska was spoken of in the present tense, as if it hadn't ceased to exist. And our summer boarding house.

The buildings here were erected quickly: post-and-beam structures, wooden boards and some pine-needle thatch inside to keep in the warm air. They still prove to be resilient, more than half a century older than their oldest inhabitants. They pretend they haven't been orphaned. They've always kept their style. Tradition and modernity in their eclectic form. Sculpted patios hidden in jasmine shrubs and window shutters with stars curved out, adorned with wild vines pruned along the frames to let the light in. Small, mezzanine terraces with outside ladders, towers, spiky spires on a scaled roof, with or without weathercock. And if not with weathercock, then with a flag. And glassed-in verandas, lounge areas with deck chairs for air cures—at that time the height of fashion. Lofty, dry rooms with large windows soaking in the sun for the Catholics and Israelites with chronic chest problems. Winter and summer rooms, on the ground floor, or above, all at an accessible price. The rooms on the first floor are cheaper because they require a hike up the stairs, but they're cozier. Everything according to the whims of the visitors in need of treatment and the summer guests, all conveniences included: tubs, showers, hot and cold water. A sophisticated cuisine, upon request dietetic, using butter. The continuous care of doctors; before each rental, the place is thoroughly disinfected. And two acres of forest. Fancy-shmancy, maybe not quite Karlsbad, but better than Ciechocinek. Paved streets, palm trees in wooden planters, gaslights, the right atmosphere and elegance. And the streets bursting with pastry shops and ice-cream vendors, buffets (organized groups receive a discount), shops with colonial foods (tea, coffee, various brands of cocoa, tobacco products), reading rooms and salons for card playing, concert halls and prayer houses, kiosks with daily newspapers and periodicals (the papers arrive with the earliest trains to be sent to subscribers twice a day) but also selling stamps and postcards with landscapes, doctor's scales, billiards, and radios!

On summer evenings, crowds of pedestrians swarmed on the path through the resort, the Warsaw gentry ambled up and down, the lanterns flickered. Couples swirled on the dance floor until everyone felt dizzy, the orchestra inviting the guests to dance the tango every night: "Take everything . . . or nothing . . ." Jauntily, as if the world weren't marching toward catastrophe. There were new romances and children were born. The owners of boarding houses counted their earnings, and the guests booked rooms for next year. Only in the hospitals, hidden away in the woods, there were patients with consumption passing away in their prime. The burial society's two-wheeled cart took away their starved corpses, wrapped in deathly shirts, took them along a wide forest track, toward the sunrise, to the house of life.

Finally, in the thicket of trees the wood edifice of the Gorewicz Boarding House appeared. It stared into the street with its dead windows, as arabesque arches watched their reflection in a dirty glass contemplating their own interminable beauty. It's almost there. The road took a sharp turn here, leaving the building on its own. At the train crossing, a hunched switch booth with rotting boards. From the chimney, a playful line of smoke rose toward the sky.

Further down, there was only the silence of a forest that exuded a scent of pinecones.

2

FROM THE GREENERY, a two-story brick pavilion emerged. It had a slightly sloping tin roof. A faded red plaque announced that the building's purpose hadn't changed. A holiday accommodation.

I haven't been here in a long time.

Behind the fence, an enclosed garden remained. Misleadingly ordinary, like many others "on the line." Just some trees, shrubs, a few concrete paths with garden lampposts, a bank of begonias interspersed with silver frost, benches. The garden always sought to be an enclave within an enclave, to be excluded from nature and history and to exist in latency, according to its own rules. As if in spite of the entire epoch, and against all that attempted to nullify it and push it, together with the house, into the past. It seemed more humid than the rest of the forest, though the pine trees that grew in the garden, russet-colored and twisted, were not any different than those on the other side of the fence. In the summer, we'd sit here in the beach chairs or folding beds or even on the soft grass covered with spiky cones. It was crowded and full of chatter. It was bursting with life.

Luckily, the gate is open. You just cross the garden and you're already on the veranda. It's just a few steps, though when I was a kid it seemed much farther.

I learned how to walk here on this path. From the gate to the veranda and from the veranda to the gate. A big excursion. And here, in one of the wire trash cans, I discovered a dead pigeon. It stared at me with open eyes. I ran away screaming and for days

I'd avoid this path. I preferred to slalom between the trees. Or putting cones in a plastic pail. Ms. Stefa taught me how to make a portrait on the ground with cones and moss. For example, a portrait of Mr. Abram. Red rowanberries are perfect for the eyes. Mr. Abram stared in a friendly manner, he had ears of leaves and green cheeks. Then it rained, and the next day, not much was left of Mr. Abram. Mr. Leon preferred carving boats out of soft pine tree bark. An activity suitable for a man. One, two. A Swiss Army knife flickered in his hands, because Mr. Leon was the only one who could carve boats. The boy will cut himself right away. He needs an occupation! When you grow up, you'll be an engineer who builds ships. We can make a mast from a twig, see. And sails. What can we use to make sails? Maybe from a newspaper, but Mr. Leon didn't like to use the paper because maybe there was something in it he still hadn't read, so my boats never got their sails, and they finally wilted away at the bottom of a bag along with an assemblage of twigs and field stones.

I marched down the path, turning my head approximately where the dead piegon had lain in the trash can. The front door is locked. The doorbell doesn't seem to work. At least I didn't manage to summon anyone. The entire building seemed to be asleep. Windows shut, nobody on the terrace, the balconies are empty. The weather uncertain, so nothing is even left to dry, the beach chairs are folded, so they won't get wet.

There is always the kitchen entrance. Feels silly—to enter from the kitchen. Like an intruder. But stick around here for an eternity?

"Who are you looking for?"

She surprised me with her question. She appeared from nowhere, though she had to have come down this path. Were the doors to the dining room slightly open? You could barely see her in her gray tweed two-piece. She resembled a wax doll. Gnarled and fragile, an arched back with protruding hips. Her permed red hair quivered anxiously like a squirrel's head, and she gave me a side-look first with one eye, then the other. She hid how pale her face was with a pink powder blush. Narrow and dry lips were painted with crimson lipstick. Over and over, she moistened them with the tip of her tongue as if she wanted to make sure they were still in the right place.

"Me? Myself," I mumbled.

"Yourself?" She was clearly agitated. "This is a boarding house."

She positioned herself in such a way that her petite frame was blocking the stairs to the porch. I pretended I didn't see them.

"I know, and I'd like to go in."

"Why do you want to come in, sir?" She was suspicious.

"I'm from here." I didn't have a better way to explain myself. "I used to live here."

"Live here? What do you mean by 'live here'? And who are you? I haven't seen you here before."

"Long ago, I was here a long time ago." This didn't come across very cleverly.

"What do you mean 'long time'? How long ago?"

"Well, a while back." I felt stupid. She stared at me even more intently. She didn't seem to believe me.

"I don't understand any of this," she shook her squirrel head, "I don't know anymore. Who said you used to live here?"

I lowered my shoulders. The old lady was not satisfied.

"I don't understand," she was disconcerted.

"So, what are we going to do now? Is it open? Is the Director in his office?"

"The Director? What Director?"

I wasn't sure if she was joking.

"Well, the headman . . ." helplessly, I opened my hands. "He's probably busy?"

"The Director?" She still didn't understand. "Oh! Him!" She figured it out. A smile covered her powdered face. "He is sitting here, in the office. You're here to see him," again she was suspicious.

"Yes," I responded flatly.

"Fine. Let me check. I'll tell him," she made a full turn and as if nothing had happened, she began to walk away.

At the end of the asphalt path, another figure appeared. Leaning on a cane and even smaller than the previous figure, in a light-colored overcoat and a linen hat sitting low to cover her ears. The only thing protruding from underneath the hat was a gnarled nose, twisted like a root. Exactly like Ms. Tecia. She had to come. A friendly soul in the garden. Inseparable from the landscape. If she weren't here, the whole garden and home would dissipate like a pure fog. She was always here. The oldest. So old that she was outside of time.

The first old lady started in her direction. I followed her. If the other one really is Ms. Tecia, I'll finally be allowed into the house. Ms. Tecia will plead my case. She will explain, vouch for me, and I'll be able to rent a room here. Everybody here knows Ms. Tecia.

Both of them ignored me.

"Mala?" Ms. Tecia spoke. Thanks to her I learned the name of the other old lady. "Where were you? I looked for you in the forest, you know?"

"I was here the whole time. I didn't move from here at all," Ms. Mala was defensive. It was obvious she feared Ms. Tecia.

"How were you here if you were not here?" Ms. Tecia gave a grim look.

The permed head arched even further back.

"How can you know if you were in the forest?"

"So, I'm telling you. This is why I went to the forest—to look for you."

"What is this? Hide-and-seek? Why were you looking for me if I was sitting here on the beach chair?"

Ms. Tecia pretended to be hurt.

"I was worried about you! Like a normal person. You left without saying a word."

"But I was here the whole time." Ms. Mala was not about to capitulate.

"Oh, stop it!" Now, Ms. Tecia was hurt for real. "Look at her, a queen!"

She continued on the path. Ms. Mala followed her, toddling two steps behind.

"I don't understand what you want. Why are you bothering me?"

Ms. Tecia didn't want to hear any excuses. Ms. Mala stopped

in the middle of the path as if she were too tired to chase her friend. She shook her head in a gesture of desperation and turned unexpectedly. It seemed that my presence made her happy this time. Was I supposed to come to her rescue? Persuade the other one that Ms. Mala was here in the garden? And what if Ms. Tecia won't believe me? Like Ms. Mala, she'd take me for an intruder? Or, come to the conclusion that I'm someone else? After all, I was also not sure if Ms. Tecia is really Ms. Tecia. Either way, intervening between them was a risky move.

Fighting old people. Mr. Leon yelling and calling Mr. Chaim a Zionist. When they stepped out to smoke on the terrace. Mr. Leon ran and danced around a three-legged iron ashtray and waved his arms violently. Mr. Chaim calmly made his seat on the bench and slowly, listening or not to Mr. Leon, fitting a cigarette into his cigarette holder. They are talking over each other, so it's hard to understand. Voices from the audience. Could you stop at least for a moment? They are arguing nonstop, as if there were something to argue over. And do you really have to smoke here? People come here specifically to breathe fresh air, you should have stayed home if you want to stink up the place. And to do it around a kid! But who told you to sit here, ma'am? They want to take away from you the last pleasure. And somewhere in the midst of this racket Ms. Tecia with a stack of fresh newspapers and a bag full of new books for Mr. Abram's library. In the same overcoat and light-colored linen hat.

The voices quieted. It seemed like I wasn't needed. The perm finally caught up with the disappearing hat. My presence did not restrain them.

"Did you see?" Ms. Mala grabbed Ms. Tecia's elbow.

"What?" The other shook her head.

"A boy came."

"What boy."

"Still young."

"Which young boy?"

"Well, he came."

"I know he came. Do you think I don't hear what you're saying to me?"

"So what now?"

"And who is he?"

"He says he's from here."

"From here? One of ours?"

"I don't know. I'm trying to tell you, he came."

They came closer together.

"I'm telling you, I know him." Ms. Tecia lowered her voice.

"Him? And how do you know him?"

"I remember him," she almost whispered. "You don't know him?" She looked at me with disappointment, as if it was my fault that Ms. Mala is seeing me for the first time in her life.

"No," the other one answered.

It seemed like the right time to say hello. Ms. Tecia had a reason to feel hurt that I had not done it yet.

"Maybe I can," I finally joined in. "Good morning, Ms. Tecia"

"You don't know?" Ms. Tecia didn't respond to my greeting. As if I were not there at all.

"No," Ms. Mala insisted.

"Well, this is Bronka's grandson. You don't recognize him?"

"Bronka's? What Bronka?"

"Well, Bronka."

"Which one? Who is she?"

"The one who passed away," Ms. Tecia tried to be specific.

"Passed away," Ms. Mala grew frightened. "How can it be that she passed away?"

"Normal, she passed away."

"Passed away!" It seemed like Ms. Mala wanted to scream something but couldn't.

I stood between them, eagerly waiting for my turn. But it wasn't coming. They continued to ignore me.

"Passed away?" She wanted to double-check. "How did she pass away? What was wrong with her?"

"Right!" Ms. Tecia opened her arms. "More than a decade ago. What can you do?"

"And she was his mother?"

"Who said she was his mother?" Ms. Tecia became frustrated. "I'm telling you, his grandmother."

"I don't know. I don't know her," Ms. Mala shook her head as if she were trying to push away my whole history. "Maybe?" She thought for a moment. "But no. How can it be that she passed away?"

"Why am I even trying to explain this to you!" Ms. Tecia evidently lost her patience. Suddenly, she turned to me.

"Do you see? And how can you talk to her? She's lost it completely! Do you understand? This is impossible!" She held me under my arm.

"She knew your grandmother, you know?" she didn't stop talking. She dug into my arm and told me to turn around as if she wanted to go back to the house already. "She remembers everything very well, but right now she isn't doing so well. She's lost her mind a little."

She stopped to size me up properly.

"Why did you come? For the company? Almost no one is left here, each week they're taking someone. I also don't know how long I will stick around. And the young ones aren't eager to come, so what will you do here? It's boring to be around old people. Come, you will walk me upstairs now."

We tottered down the path. The doors were open.

3

THE FIRST-FLOOR room was quite large, though smaller than it seemed at first. Four or five steps from the door to the window, three or four from the freestanding closet to the stool. A room like any other room, what else to expect in a boarding house of this quality? All rooms are the same, save for the view—either the garden or the backyard. Better the garden. The view is better, and it's nicer, because you can't smell the kitchen and at night you can't hear the dog barking in the neighboring lot. Yet, there was something uncanny about this room. If you peaked into it through a keyhole, it narrowed, like a kaleidoscope toward the window, or more precisely, the balcony door that was so wide that even with semi-opaque curtains the entire room filled with strong afternoon light. An ordinary box-shaped, though slightly crooked—most likely the bricklayer lost control of his level while truing the walls. The side wall's pale, distemper-yellow paint was a futile effort to cover fungus that had grown over the previous layers of paint. The walls slightly inclined as if their secret desire was one day to collapse on a man living here. Yet, in the near future, the real danger was probably looming from a tiny chandelier put together from small wood blocks with two light bulbs screwed into them. Attached to the ceiling, the contraption, worn out by time, wobbled in the wind that entered the room through the slightly ajar transom window. In any case, let it fall, it's useless, and the light so poor that it can only worsen your sight. You have problems with reading. As soon as you open a book, your eyes close. And when you fall asleep, you wake up immediately, because there is no air or the opposite—it's as cold as an outdoor doghouse and so on.

An iron bed covered with a wool blanket in red and gray plaid. The blanket, worn out from being folded in four all these years, was adorned with a purple text stamped in the corner: "Boarding Ho . . ." Another similar blanket, but in washed-out gray-burgundy, poked out from underneath a small pillow in a white cover with a similar text, but this time in green. Pillows in boarding houses are always a little too small as if the service people were parsimonious in their distribution of feathers or kapok. Kapok, because feathers are expensive. In the old days, duvets filled with down were given to the bride as a wedding gift. The whole family chipped in, so the young couple could lie on something soft when finally together. And now? Doctors say that large pillows are not good for your back and it's better to sleep on something flat. But you will always have enough time to sleep on flat surfaces. You will sleep for all times' sake.

Ms. Tecia stood in the middle of her kingdom. She was fragile, almost disappearing behind a table not much shorter than her, the top crowded with medicine bottles and piles of newspapers. The newspapers with notes in the margins. Just the way it used to be in our house. Countless piles, each held together with twine, with a note on ruled paper: January, February. March, April . . . the previous year, and a pile from three years ago. Disappearing in the thicket of it all, growing smaller and smaller, there was the owner holding the black magnifying glass she used in an attempt to decipher her archaic notes. Home archives, dusty reams of yellow paper shoved in every corner. Important articles! A whole life of collecting. Porcelain sets. Treasures that were never used. It's a waste to use them, but it's a shame to throw them away. They might come in handy, if not now, maybe one day. And who knows what comes next? We're not wealthy enough to waste. Electrolux vacuum cleaner with a brass plate and a rubber hose dead for forty years now. A rusty kettle, and a mattress with holes rolled up and hurled into the overhead storage, a shearling with moth holes packed into a bag made of a stitched-together sheet. And on the very bottom, grandmother's green Polish army uniform and a side cap with an eagle, which she wore once in a picture. Rags in boxes, organized: linen and cotton, nylon and rayon. For sewing and the more damaged ones for carding. Also winter and summer clothes in separate cardboard boxes, never opened, because what for? And yarn for sweaters, moths shamelessly emerging from colorful balls of yarn, making a few anxious rounds around the storeroom before quickly returning to their cotton nests, discouraged by the stink of naphthalene and lavender. Objects that have more life than people. Now abandoned. Who will put them back, so they don't drift about atop some garbage dump? You bury holy books, why not have a funeral for a used pair of shoes? They say that's what Mendel from Kock did.

Ms. Tecia opened her hands helplessly and took large breaths as if each breath were her last.

"See how we live here? I'm telling you, this place is unbearable. You pay so much and what? You save all year long, and then you have to go out into the hallway to pee. And there is a draft because the windows are not properly sealed. They were supposed to fix this, but they didn't. It's always a waste to spend money on old people. It's better to build a mansion for yourself, like the woman in the kitchen. But let me tell you, I'm not complaining. And your grandma wasn't complaining either. I am not bourgeois! In our generation, there was no room for complaint. One was glad to have anything. You know how hard it is to get a single room here? Mrs. Szrajer tried, Marysia Fuksowa, too—nothing. And I was lucky this year! Doctor Askanas says that this isn't luxury of any kind, a tiny room with no bathroom. Ma'am, you deserve it for the years you put in, he teases me. But tell me, why would I need more? Sit, here is a chair for you. The room is such a mess!"

And yet, something drew them here. To this dingy boarding house with its perpetually peeling plaster. They were home. At least here, behind the fence. It's not such an easy or trivial thing to have a home. Not all were afforded it. That's what Mr. Chaim said. We're never home, permanent wanderers, like on the relief in the back of the Monument to the Ghetto Heroes, where a rabbi with a Torah leads the crowd. Otherwise, why did Moses lead the Exodus from Egypt? Was it so bad for him there? Is it better now?

I sat at the table. Ms. Tecia on the bed.

"See?" she pointed at the wall. "It's from Bronka. Pretty."

A brown graphic print. Jerusalem. Montefiore. A landscape with a windmill and the King David hotel. Misshapen houses and whitewashed walls. Joel Rohr, a graphic artist, Yemin Moshe. He spoke in Yiddish, so my grandma could understand him. Ma'am, are you from Poland? There are still Jews in Poland? Cousin Yakov drove me there in his Subaru, long ago, right after Shabbat. Cousin Yakov is religious like the rest of the family. You will come, we will find you a school, you'll learn Hebrew. What will you do there? You can write here, as well. Old Town, Mount Sinai, illuminated with orange floodlights. Tisha B'Av was coming, fasting to commemorate the destruction of the Temple. Everything soaked in the scent of boxwood, myrtle and rhododendron giving you a headache. And then the sound of cicadas and the swishing of garden sprinklers in air still warm after a hot day. In the summer, in the evening even a light breeze is rare. Today I remember this first sight and that scent, even though I've stood in that place by the windmill at least another fifty times.

"And this? You know it, right?"

The twelve tribes of Israel. Chagall and his stained-glass windows in the Hadassah Hospital. More mysterious in their reproductions than there, shot through with the Jerusalem light. The tribe of Simeon, over a desk in an office. I could stare at it for hours. Silvery globe and flying horses against a navy blue sky. Divided in Jacob, scattered in Israel. Twelve images, each in a different house. Good for a gift. Brown Judah with a ram, green Issachar, canary yellow Levi with Moshe's Tables and the Star of David suspended between two birds. A token of the Land in a Jewish house, instead of a mezuzah. Something to connect to the next year in Jerusalem. Like a brass Hannukah lamp at Uncle Motia's, never used, on the wall in the living room. Remorse.

"Now I'll show you something you don't know. See what I've got here. Do you want to know?"

Under a pile of newspapers from last month, of course only the most important ones because Ms. Tecia never kept superfluous papers in the room, there was a cardboard shoebox with a label: Chełmek pumps, brown. It was tied in a cross with a pink ribbon made from a rotting fabric.

"I have it here. I hid it. Help me take it out. So many documents burned! We were walking out of Warsaw, you know? And Bronka took it with her. Come, sit here for a moment."

Like the rabbi with a Torah from the Ghetto Monument. What can you carry out from a burning city? And where to take it? Maybe it's better not to have it? The memory—jolted, unable to rest in peace, later weighs you down like a stone. And those who didn't rescue anything look on with envy at the few odds and ends that my grandma hid in her coat pocket back then.

Ms. Tecia untied a ribbon and lifted the lid. Inside, tightly packed, one next to the other, little paper wraps rested. They resembled paper mummies, as if their owners never left the house of bondage: each wrap bundled in paper and secured with a rubber band, the bigger ones with two rubber bands crossed, just in case, who knows what can happen?

"Just don't mix them up!" Ms. Tecia warned me, "Actually, let me show you."

In the first wrap, under a layer of newspaper, rests the next one. How many years ago? It's easy to check the date. The *Warsaw Life Daily*, "Deliberation of Voivodeship activists," "Report from Comrade K." This was wrapped ages ago. Each such wrap is a miniature paradise for an archaeologist.

One more newspaper. "The Peace Marathon on the Streets of the Capitol." And finally. First, a gray envelope, then a few smaller ones with a cellophane layer. Postcards.

"Everything is fuzzy. My sight is poor. You look."

Thick, yellowed paper. The Royal Castle in an elegant sepia, in front of it trees that were not replanted when it was reconstructed. A lanky Prudential building, the first and last pre-war skyscraper, flexes gladly on the Warecki Square, towering over the roofs of eclectic walkups on Świętokrzyska, the street of rare and used bookstores. And a gracious lady, in a hat and bright spring outfit, traverses a smooth sidewalk. In a moment, she will take a turn on Szpitalna. Black Fords, Peugeots, and Fiats flash their lights. In the Saski Garden, a colonnade ending with a white, goblet-shaped fountain. A few couples in love sit on benches, above them chestnut trees with drooping leaves, you can reach them, they will blossom soon. Greetings from Warsaw, it's not clear from whom, the Parisian addressee also unknown. Sharp, masculine handwriting. In Polish. A lawyer or a doctor. A wedding announcement, no, actually an announcement of a honeymoon, at least that's what it seems like from the context. An annotation in feminine handwriting, affectionately yours. A zigzag instead of a signature. And warm greetings from Paris, but possibly sent to someone else, to Świętojerska; actually sent to us, the message scrawled by Mr. Tov, a family friend, from Muranów. First, he collected rags from the streets, but in time he made so much money from it that he had his own employees and could afford to eat at the best restaurants near the grand boulevards. I think, thirty years later, definitively after the war, he showed my grandma Montmartre. Her portrait in chalk from the Place du Tertre has long faded.

How did these papers end up with Ms. Tecia? "I don't know. I don't remember. We gathered everything that was left after the war"—I think she began to regret that she showed me her box. She was not in a mood to provide explanations. I could tell from the look on her face.

In the second wrap there were letters, wartime letters, addressed in Warsaw and sent to Łuck. (Because the ones sent from Łuck to Warsaw, of course, are gone.) How is it possible that back then, against all odds, the post office still worked and was still sending letters? After all, they must have known what would happen to the senders in a year or six months. An oversight, or were they lying until the end?

Either way, only single words are left, scattered here and there. It's hard to decipher anything, as if they were written not in ink but in onion juice. And in the place of each faded letter, evil is nesting, is it not? And each crippled serif, broken tail, crooked crown of Shin, even if crevices between ascenders are the size of a hair, don't they move and shake the foundation of the universe and take away a piece of its existence?

"Can you see anything?" Ms. Tecia looked over my shoulder again. Her face covered with worry. "You can't see anything anymore."

I nodded.

"I knew this would happen," she groaned. "They've been here for so long! The whole family history! And your grandma's, too. Adam, my nephew, was supposed to make a copy, but he's always busy. We should take it to the archives, but they will lose it there for sure. Better if it stays here . . ."

Without waiting for permission, I took the rubber bands off the next wrap. From underneath the three layers of papers, cut into even squares, the next pile of letters poked out. All of it like an Egyptian papyrus, remnants of letters on tissue paper. Letters, possibly post-war letters, in Yiddish, mixed in with electricity bills, because all documents should be stored, who knows what will prove useful? Letters written with a fountain pen in a longhand that nobody uses anymore. Who can still read them?

I sat there for an hour, paying no attention to Ms. Tecia and trying to decipher the contents of consecutive wraps. The room was steeping in dusk, but I didn't feel like getting up to turn the mini-chandelier on. The letters in the letters, almost illegible, were melting in the twilight. They were disappearing with each moment. In places where even a moment before I was able to see their shapes, and even tried to put words back together, to catch their basic sense in whatever language, the emptiness of ragged parchment paper now spread. Thus, I took off consecutive rubber bands, ripping consecutive layers of paper that crumbled upon touch as if under the weight of the words that were once printed on them. At first, each sheet of letter paper trembled in my fingers, leaving the impression that a particle of forgotten life still smoldered within. Each sheet I turned around in my hands and then lifted up seeking the last bits of daylight still coming through the lace curtains. I stared intently and squinted hard, attempting to read the slanted sentences, but the sheet was collapsing inwardly, fading faster and turning black until I wasn't able to see anything.

"I'm too tired," Ms. Tecia whispered. Some time ago, though I didn't even notice when, she slowly moved along the windowsill trying to rest against it until she lay down, or actually fell down on her bed in a semi-standing position as if she planned to continue to sit and chat with me. She breathed quietly. I walked up to her to take a plaid blanket from underneath the pillow and tightly wrap it round her tiny and frail body.

"Don't worry about me. You can sit here. I'm not sleeping yet. Stay," she asked.

I fixed her pillow. Ms. Tecia asked me to place it edge up.

"You should also look at the photos. Very interesting."

The next shoebox had also been tied with a ribbon. The knot didn't give way easily under my fingers, but the box finally opened. Inside, there were wraps similar to the ones in the previous box, though maybe slightly more flattened and less like mummies. I took the first one out, then another. An intricate inner arrangement immediately fell apart.

"Don't look at them now." A shy tone of request made itself heard in Ms. Tecia's voice. She wanted me to give her a break and leave. "Take them with you. I don't want to have them here with me."

I was almost glad. I threw the wraps back into the box in no particular order. I couldn't close it. I tied it with the last bits of the ribbon.

Ms. Tecia gave a loud sigh. I was taking her treasure from her.

"It's good that you came." She smiled slightly. "But now I have to go to sleep. Before supper. See, I'm not fit anymore for work. Good, go."

4

THE HALLWAY AND the dining room were suspended in the dusky wait for evening. Only the clicking of a typewriter coming from a poorly lit office next to the common room signaled that life in the boarding house had not been extinguished. The Director is completing his daily tasks. Stewardship, utilities, produce, detergent, light bulbs that need to be changed on the second floor. Knocking on the door breaks his attention.

"May I?"

"Please, come in."

"I was supposed to come," I began hesitatingly.

"Oh, yes . . ." the Director looked at me, suspicious.

"Right."

"Give me a moment." He looked at the guest list. "What do we have here for you? Right . . . Good. For how long? Would you kindly sign here," he passed me the registration book. "Good. And the date. Today is Thursday. We need to keep things in order."

He collapsed into his armchair.

"If I may ask . . ." he vacillated as if he were searching for a word that could most precisely express his curiosity, "are you a . . ."

"Yes."

He let out a sigh of relief.

"How's Warsaw? You know, sir, this place is a bit of a hide-away. We depend on the mercy of visitors or on the lack of it, away from the madness. Swindlers, they all just score wins for

20

themselves, no one's thinking about others. They think they're better! Anyway, you're probably tired."

"Not really."

We sat there for a moment in silence, eyeing each other. The Director of the holiday resort and his office. Holiday resort. An exaggerated label. In the old days, it was called "a boarding house," but "a boarding house" is too bourgeois. Birkat haBayt, a blessing for the house written on a decorative cardboard hangs above the desk. This wasn't here before. It's in the place of the Issac Leib Peretz portrait. Or maybe it was Sholem Aleichem? Serious faces. Only the biggest ones, the classics of Yiddish literature, were taken to be hung on the mezzanine floor.

"Let's go eat," he offered. "Supper is waiting. Others have already eaten; it's late. They prefer to eat earlier, at six. So, they can rest before the evening news. Seven thirty, the holy hour. If a rabbi held services, he'd have a full house. It's just that they prefer to sit in front of their TVs. That kind of prayer, at least no one is bothering God. Anyway, we had a rabbi here, years ago, he came from the United States. He met with us, and you know what, nobody wanted to pay attention to him. What do they care about a rabbi, here everyone thinks they're a rabbi. And women—a rebbetzin. Is that a problem? In their generation? But they have forgotten, so much time has passed. Since we've installed TV sets in the rooms, they only show up for meals. Sometimes not even for that. The common room is a thing of the past."

The common room with a clumsy fresco, behind the dining room. I used to think it was a ballroom and that's what I called it. Separated by a heavy, semi-circular door. Crystal glass framed in wood. Hard to peek in, the space was always filled with sacral dusk. The most mysterious place in the house. It was set aside for adults, but I was allowed to come there for evening cartoons. Before the news. White noise on the screen of the color TV that no one knew how to tune properly. I'm sitting alone in a dark room, and next to me, in an upholstered, plush armchair Mr. Chaim is whistling. Old, wise Mr. Chaim! Everybody went to see him, he gave advice to anyone who asked for it. During the day, the common room filled with talk. A black grand piano, the bridge corner, zeks un zechcyg, what's new in the *Folks Shtime*? Politics, books, Rudnicki wrote a new piece. In the old days, it was always better, that's the way the world works.

All of this seen through crystal glass. Heads, one next to the other, on folding club chairs they're listening to a reading. In front of them, a tall man explains something. His hands are raised, intensely gesticulating. His eyes are glistening. The door-knob is at eye level, maybe even higher. Many years later, a New Year's Eve party. The ballroom, now in its intended role, is covered in confetti and streamers. Balloons suspended on strings float above the dining room, the tables pushed together, covered with a white tablecloth. Evening gowns and double-breasted suits. Vodka from a local store, no dance band, but the rest of it just like the old days of going out to dance. And once again, the ballroom, more recently. A makeshift synagogue at a Jewish youth camp. The holy ark made from a cabinet covered with a drape. Playing tag to catch boys for the morning minyan. They wake me up after 8 a.m., dragged from bed, I trudge like a sleep-walker. Without the other ten, the Almighty won't hear the three who want him to hear them. Although it's summer, it's cold, I sit receding in the back, trying to catch up with the prayer leader. The sacred, somehow, having escaped.

I peeled my nose from the glass. It's closed, I can't get in.

They turned the sconce light on in the dining room. The dusk sneaked through the five veranda windows. The Director pointed to a seat at the staff table. A silent waitress placed on it a breadbasket and plates for me. A heavy white set, coffee pots made of thick porcelain. The mandatory set of spices: salt, pepper, Maggi seasoning and white vinegar in cruets of thick glass.

The Maggi seasoning is great on mashed potatoes. What is white vinegar for? Pork chops? Not a kosher resort, peasant, cafeteria food. You won't get a taste of bouillon with farfalle here; carrots and peas in batter to substitute tzimmes. A chicken dish without dry plums isn't a chicken. The whole point of koshering is to keep Jews from mingling with goyim. And how much good did it do? Has anyone seen a Jewish chef?

"It's quiet here, isn't it?" The Director tried to make small talk. "Dead air."

I nodded.

"This time of the year, almost no one is here, not like it used to be. In the summer, it's so-so. And now? A coal man, a cleaning lady. And us."

"Well, what about . . ." I protested.

"Oh, them!" He waved his hand armed with a fork. "They're always here, so it's like they aren't here. In the old days, the place was busy! Back then, there were still Jews."

Silence fell over us.

In the old days, the meals were announced with a wooden-handled hand bell. The prerogative of children. You stood near the dining room, on steep, linoleum stairs in the hall with spruce paneling. The best spot for the sound to carry. Two minutes to one. It was a real honor and a great responsibility. The vacationers are marching to the dining room. Mr. Leon with inseparable Mr. Abram. They were always fighting. Mr. Chaim. Ms. Tecia, Ms. Rosa, Dr. Kaminska with her quiet sister. And the blind writer from the ground floor—Mr. Dawid, who always climbed slowly up the steps leading to the terrace. And there was one more gentleman, very old; every year, he took the room facing the backyard. They said he didn't have a hand, but I did see his palm—always in a black glove. He never took it off among strangers. Either way, I was scared of him.

A big spotted dog that up until now had been napping in the corner moved anxiously, raised his head to listen, but sensing a familiar scent, went back to sleep. Someone standing outside pushed a wing of the half-open door. In the doorway, a dark silhouette appeared.

"Peace to this house!"

An older man swiftly walked across the dining room.

"Jakub! Hallo!" the Director seemed glad to see him. "What are you doing here? Did you not get dinner? Come over, please meet our guest. Sir, do you know Jakub?"—it was a confirmation more than a question. "Jakub, he is our old regular."

"Very old," Mr. Jakub corrected him, coughed theatrically.

This isn't the first time I've seen his bold skull wrapped in parchment skin so thin that it could rip under the slightest touch. Protuberant cheekbones and blushing cheeks—he rushed to get here. Walking down the stairs also requires effort. Bluish veins on his temples pulsated unattractively. I was trying to retrieve his face from a hidden corner of my mind, to restore it from that corner as if from a very imperfect photographic film, to retouch it and fill in the details, which I now had in front of me. And then to recover everything else—his name and his place on the social map.

A futile effort. No countenance stored in my memory fit the face of the stranger. And yet I was sure that Mr. Jakub wasn't really a stranger. Frankly speaking, he didn't seem like a stranger at all. Clearly, he was someone who existed, who had to exist. If not now, at least back then.

"I think I know our young companion," Mr. Jakub proudly stated. "Our young companion used to holiday here, would sit here with us at the table."

In the sidelight of sconces, the discoloration on his low forehead looked like some bizarre growth.

"How long do you plan to stay here?"

"A few days."

"A few days. En route? I understand. A short stay. Youth is always on the move."

His protruding, curious eyes were piercing through me. Do I remember him? Back then on the terrace? A gentleman in a photograph. I'm two years old. I sit in a stroller, and I'm chatting with someone who possibly resembles Mr. Jakub. Me alone and them. The only child, I never had any peers here.

"You do look like yourself," admitted Mr. Jakub, sounding like someone who knows everything. As if he's just left my own thoughts.

"And what brings you here?" The Director tried to join the conversation.

"As they say, same old Jewish poverty. If you're a Jew, you want to sit among your own."

"Not many people are left, fewer and fewer," the Director sighed. "There are more and more of them everywhere else in the world and it's the opposite around here."

"That's the Jewish thing, always against the grain," Mr. Jakub observed in a mildly sarcastic tone. "Step outside the tent. How many stars! Remember our Patriarch, Abraham?"

"I will multiply thy seed as the stars of heaven," suggested the Director. "Am I right?"

"You can see many of them this year."

"Like every year, Jakub. Stars aren't like people, they don't wane and are not missed. But don't look up at the sky—look around."

Mr. Jakub looked at the younger man with indulgence. What does he want? What happened cannot be reversed. How long can you beat the drum, wailing? Your whole life? Or even longer? Until the skin on the drum breaks.

The Director could not calm down, some inner turmoil consumed him. He was almost ready to explode.

"Now, they come out of their mouseholes. For forty years, they weren't Jewish. What am I saying, not since birth, and now, here you go, he's a full on Jew, and his son—in Israel, suddenly very religious."

"You will have more people coming in. Ours, not ours, what difference does it make to you? He's paying for his bed, and that's it."

"And it doesn't make any difference to you?!" the Director shouted. He got up from the table abruptly. "I'm done, do you understand?! What is this place? Not a hospital, not a morgue! All of it topsy-turvy. Thirty years ago . . ."

"You don't need to school me on what it was like thirty years ago! What's thirty years? Do you know what this place looked like before the war?"

"No. And I don't want to know." The Director, offended, started toward the door.

"Don't pay attention to him, sir." Mr. Jakub turned to me and whispered in confidence: "This is his usual spiel. An old fool! The Director. He's a big director now, but he used . . . Anyway, why am I even telling you this, it's a waste to worry over it now."

"Director, is it true that instead of saying 'good evening,' it's common now to say 'hallo'?"

The Director stopped halfway. All three of us turned our heads. Rosy cheeks and a brown perm. Ms. Mala. None of us noticed her earlier. She snuck in unnoticed and just like that she began to eat her supper.

"I don't know," he growled.

"Young people use it," Mr. Jakub explained to her.

The Director, grinding his teeth, stepped out of the dining room.

"What happened to him?" she asked.

"Same as always." Mr. Jakub waved his hand condescendingly.

"Right!" She seemed slightly surprised. "And the boy, he came here with you?"

"No." Now Mr. Jacob was surprised. "What are you talking about? Why? This isn't his first time, he's been here before."

"Before—what do you mean before?" she could not follow. "He just arrived here. We went for a walk with Tecia and suddenly he's here. And do you know each other?" She would not give up.

"The world is small. And the Jewish world even smaller. We all know one another."

"I don't follow. The boy came and what is he going to do here?"

"I don't follow you, ma'am? How is it your business? He came and here he is."

"Good! You are not in a chatty mood today." She took offense.

"What can you do?"

"You better show the boy his room. The room where they used to live. The cleaning woman has already changed the sheets."

"Thank you. I can go alone, I'll find my way."

5

THE SHIMMERING LIGHT of the wall lamps in the dining room didn't reach far. The mezzanine floor window breathed darkness and gushing bits of wind pushed through the cracks. Twilight was rather thick in the first floor hallway. I groped through, holding the walls. A small house, but no help in sight. This was probably why Mr. Daniel preferred to stick to the ground floor. At least he didn't risk falling down the stairs.

The floor, although it was covered with a soft carpet, made squeaky sounds that broke the billowing silence. My hand finally reached a light switch. A gray lampshade responded with the scant light of a fluorescent lamp. Dried dead flies cast fantastically-shaped shadows. Considering the size of the building, the hallway was short, yet it seemed to lengthen as I crossed it. I used to be scared of walking down here: over there, at the end, a damp and stuffy twilight draped with a thin layer of dust particles that reluctantly parted in front of an intruder. But maybe the source of my fears was entirely different, I'm not sure anymore. It is very likely that I feared less the darkness and more the consequences of illicit ventures into the regions whose existence for reasons still unclear was kept from me like a deep secret.

This darkness was filled with a mawkish smell of sweetness and ammoniac mixed in equal measure with a strong scent of medications. I strangely enjoyed this disconcerting chemical note oozing out of half-opened bottles. An uncanny scent of tranquility and gravity hinting at the border of the adult's sphere where people were focused on themselves and their medicine.

I remember Mr. Chaim sitting down on a shaky stool and patiently waiting for the water to boil in his enameled mug. He dissolved in it a straw-colored concoction: the liquid boiled for a moment, spitting with a hissing sound bubbles that whirled on the surface until Mr. Chaim stopped them with a firm tap of an aluminum teaspoon. Then he gulped it in one draft. A few quick slurps, two or three coughs, and it's done. Just a handful of multicolored pills: oblong drops in shiny coating and white tablets of different thicknesses and diameters. There were so many of the latter that I could not fathom how Mr. Chaim was able to control this chaos or how he distinguished between them. I can't rule out the possibility that all of his pills contained the same ingredient that on an unexplained whim was divided into batches. Maybe this was done simply to insert for Mr. Chaim some variety into long and monotonous boarding house days.

The sweet fusty smell, the result of an agglomeration of panaceas, a concentration of medicine as well as a persistent aversion to airing the rooms, intensified with each year, with each moment. It penetrated walls, becoming one with particles of plaster, and nothing could draw it out of there. It probably evaporated just now together with a small group of this place's most devoted guardians.

I walked and walked, passing by shiny pairs of doors on each side. The fastened, numbered doorplates didn't want to reveal who is staying in rooms that used to be kept wide-open. I could sneak in on all fours unnoticed and poke about freely as long as I didn't venture into Ms. Hanka's room. I think she didn't like me or anyone else and just looked sternly at others in her tinted glasses. More and more, she resembled an owl. When bothered, she liked to scream loudly so the whole house could hear her hoarse and unpleasant voice:

"Children should be kept on a leash. One cannot have peace even for a moment!"

In these situations, Ms. Tecia had to intervene:

"Why are you picking on a child? What does he do to bother you?"

They didn't like each other much, though everyone here

found Ms. Tecia agreeable. And I was never afraid of Ms. Tecia, I also appreciated that she always managed to be around when Ms. Hanka was about to start voicing her many complaints against the world.

So, I was running away from Ms. Hanka, from her glasses, from her screams—to the next room, to the smiling Doctor Kahn, who, naturally, was bigger than me, yet still very tiny, even smaller than Mr. Leon. Slightly hunched, he always wore a plaid jacket made from beige wool. Doctor Kahn had a tiny bird head with a crest of gray hair at the top. He also had a beak instead of a nose, like my Uncle Motia. Glasses in gold frames, which I've later seen only on doctors, rested on it. I cherished the time at Doctor Kahn's looking through his thick books. My favorite was the leather-bound anatomy atlas where gouged-out organs were gleaming with blood, sack-shaped stomachs, oblong pancreases, ballooned livers squeezed above the maze of yellow gut. I traced the latter with my finger trying to find direction in this illogical mass, but time after time, I'd lose my way in the cluster of remarkably interconnected pipes, kinks, elbows, and folds. Thus, before I managed to reach the end of the maze, I had to start the game over. Indomitable, I would open the atlas to a random page, to track eagerly, for example, the circular system. Red and blue arteries and veins entwined all, important and not so much, nooks and crannies of the body, clustering, branching, and forming boughs, to finally reach the heart from which they sprouted out again, ceaselessly pumping a few liters of fresh, clean blood.

There was another reason, much more prosaic, why I appreciated Doctor Kahn. A bowl of hard candy stuck together in a lump waited for me in his room. Large, pink with white filling, I was allowed to take as many pieces of candy as I wanted because Doctor Kahn seemed to have inexhaustible amounts of them, or maybe he never ate them but just kept the candy for me. My Uncle Motia also kept hard candy on his desk in a glass ashtray, but he would portion out just one for me whereas Doctor Kahn would even give me a few for the road. Thus, I really liked Doctor Kahn, also for the one time when I was sick and he came in a white lab coat, auscultated me with a stethoscope, and gave me medicine from his portable first aid kit. As they say, it will heal before the wedding, our young comrade! Doctor Kahn knew how to make everyone smile, even Mr. Abram when they played chess. I don't think they always agreed, but when Mr. Abram raised his voice, Doctor Kahn responded with a joke and soon they would both laugh loudly. I wanted to heal people when I grew up and to be like Doctor Kahn, who knew so much, and could list from memory epithelial in the throat and small bones in the ear, and who used to say that a man is a miraculous machine, but a very bad soul resides in him. This last point was something that Doctor Kahn wasn't willing to explain to me, he simply stared at me with his sad dark eyes, but I could feel that there was some essential reason why he acted this way.

Doctor Kahn, Ms. Hanka, Ms. Pela, and Ms. Ziuta, they stuck together. A small band of friends—I only grasped it later, because back then, here, this was the whole world, after all, no other existed. Ms. Pela had gray hair styled tightly and fastened to her head with bobby pins. I was allowed to call her by name. Her husband, Jurek, Świętojerska 14, near Ciasna, admitted my grandma into the organization. The dark-haired Bronka, the best pair of legs in their party cell. He was an experienced comrade, a former member of KZMP, the Young Communist League of Poland, with a sentence under his belt. Tall, handsome and light-haired, talkative, a would-be lawyer—girls fell for him in droves.

So, they ran with boxes of flyers to factories, to foremen and workers, to the Brodno and Wola Districts. They did it for the cause and for his soft and sometimes stern glances, confusing their routes for the plainclothes men and returning to their headquarters at Świętojerska 14, the underground space, where Jurek gave more orders in his velvet voice. Ms. Pela mentioned him often, so did my grandma. And Ms. Ziuta did, too, though I don't think she even belonged to the organization. But Ms. Ziuta spoke English, so when I was a little older, I would quiz her for words, and Ms. Ziuta patiently wrote them down for me in a graph-ruled notebook. Next to each word, she knew to draw something that would help me remember. Ms. Ziuta was close with the Attorney—what was his name? Kirszenberg. No, of course, Attorney Kirszenberg, the one who used to live in Nowolipki, emigrated to Israel before I was born. So, it had to be a different lawyer, I'm not sure anymore. He resembled Mr. Jakub, bald like a knee, rosy cheeks, he took me for walks in the forest. And when we went to the sea the two of us, me and the lawyer whose name I can no longer remember, took long walks along a sandy beach. We walked for miles, before the evening, as the waves threw to the shore tiny seashells and the sun was setting behind the horizon and the lighthouse began sweeping the coast with a shaft of yellow light. My grandma and Aunt Guta, right behind us, discussed their secret matters, and my uncle the lawyer told me many funny stories that have all sadly evaporated from my memory.

The hallway was winding. The second wing of the building. Another row of doors. Ms. Tecia's room tightly locked, next to, I assume, Ms. Mala's room. She reminded me of someone. She looked like Ms. Wiera, but Ms. Wiera never came here. Maybe I'm wrong, but no, right . . . Ms. Wiera left after March, that's what they said, to Haifa. She went together with Mr. Witek, who like Doctor Kahn was a doctor and who had a full laugh when engaged with a party at his table. Mr. Witek knew Grandma and Grandpa from Russia when they all fled east, far away from Hitler and his gang of bandits. And probably because they escaped then, Gomułka[1] was able to kick out Mr. Witek from Warsaw, and Mr. Witek was able to take me in his car to tour a Bahá'í Shrine, which had a dome shimmering above the city with its gold scales.

And here is my room, with the same large iron-frame bed and plaid blanket as Ms. Tecia's. It has a view of the garden. But it's underlit, like others rooms, and it is rather damp, especially on cold, rainy days, and there were plenty of those. Adjacent, shared shower rooms and toilets. Mold on a taupe wall and water dripping from the ceiling. A slippery wooden drain in the shower's stone floor. A stool so you can place a soap holder, or without

---

1 Władysław Gomułka—Polish communist leader; the First Secretary of the Polish United Workers' Party in the 1950s and 1960s.

a stool if somebody took it out to the balcony. All behind a skimpy wax-cloth curtain. Two lines to the shower, men in one line, women in a separate one. A black triangle and a black circle painted on the doors. Even today I'm not sure why they use a circle and triangle. Through the keyhole, you can see Mr. Leon, or maybe Mr. Chaim in a thick white bathrobe with dark blue stripes. Camp garb. Don't say this, these are very bad words, Mr. Chaim would be very upset if he heard you! A forbidden place. Not for little kids. So, I'm standing covered in soap in the middle of the room, in a tin tub and shake from the cold. Water is splashed everywhere. The coil is not enough, the heater doesn't work correctly, you have to bring water from the boiler or the kitchen where it can be heated up on a hot plate. The luxury! Has anyone seen such a mess? To keep the elderly in such conditions! I was maybe five years old when I marched into the Director's office to complain about the mattress with holes. Come on, you can't lie on this! I walked down, through all the hallways and the dining room, and I knocked to enter and present my case. Mom was so embarrassed, the whole building gossiped about the incident, but they changed our mattresses.

One time I slipped into the men's bathroom to see this mysterious world. Mr. Henryk, an older man who lived on the second floor but who usually showered on the first floor. Hot water comes on faster and with greater pressure.

"Come, let me show you something. A toothbrush, have you seen anything like it?"

It looked much different than mine. In fact, it wasn't good for brushing teeth. It looked like a duck-shaped scrub brush. Mr. Henryk used it to polish a strange metal object that he rinsed under running water and then put into his mouth.

"You don't have anything like this yet? You still have your own teeth, right, kid?"

On the other hand, Mr. Leon also had them. Dentures. When he didn't need them, he kept them in a glass. Sometimes he even fought with Mr. Abram without his teeth in. Mr. Leon used to say that he lost his real teeth during the war, in Siberia. Before the war, Mr. Leon and my grandpa were imprisoned at

Wronki. They were in the same cell. Not for too long—though everybody was sentenced to a few years in prison, the prisoners were rotated from cell to cell to make sure they didn't grow close. They spoke a lot. Loyal comrades, tough, faithful to their ideals, devoted to the cause. The kind that come through even in the toughest times. During an underground action, they will not snitch on anyone, during an interrogation, they won't betray the Party. After the war, when my grandpa was no longer here, because he was killed in action, Mr. Leon was sent to Lublin to work on propaganda. He wrote articles and reports there. I suppose they weren't too happy with him because soon he was transferred elsewhere. Mr. Leon's daughter emigrated to Sweden, just like Mr. Abram's son, and Ms. Guta and the lawyer's kids, who used to take me to the sea; and Ms. Ania's daughter, who brought me my first potty from Stockholm.

"All the young ones spread around the world. Only the old ones stayed," Mr. Abram used to say.

Mr. Abram lost his entire family during the war. In the camps and in the ghetto. Only his son survived, and that's it. He was little, so they managed to hide him somewhere. With the farmers. Good people. Then the son left. Mr. Abram stayed.

"Someone has to be the guardian of bones," he repeated firmly.

Mr. Abram had no family, nor did Mr. Leon. Doctor Kahn lost his wife, a long time ago—I think also during the war. Mr. Chaim was also alone. Ms. Tecia had had a husband, but he was gone. Ms. Irena's husband was killed, and her son was executed in Cracow where he was hiding. Doctor Kaminska walked out of the ghetto, in Warsaw, together with her sister, on Aryan papers; they had a different last name before. I'm not sure how they survived the rest of the war. Mr. Bialer was a guerrilla, a Soviet guerrilla fighter, so he didn't return until after the war. He had a slug in his hip, and he limped slightly. Because of that slug, long ago he got compensation and a higher combatants' pension. In the lapel of a light army jacket he wore a pin with a miniature medal. For prowess. Ms. Marysia had a number on her arm, the one from Auschwitz, it was on the inside of her arm, so it wasn't always visible. But one time I saw it: It was summer, we were sitting in a garden, and Ms. Marysia wore a summer dress in a cheerful floral print. She was not embarrassed by this number, but she wouldn't let me touch it though I was very tempted. I was curious how it was made. Dark ink dots on the skin, or something along those lines? The Nazis gave people these numbers when you went to the camp. That's all Ms. Marysia wanted to tell me. I've heard that she has never told anyone what happened to her there.

Mrs. Grynsztajn and my grandma were the only ones who still had brothers, though they lived far away. Mrs. Grynsztajn's brother left before the war, first to France and from there to the United States. He never returned to Poland. Mrs. Grynsztajn would visit him there once in a while until his death.

When Mr. Abram was very old and coughed a lot, he began to work on a dictionary. A biographical dictionary of all Jews who once lived in Poland. He wrote his entries on tram tickets and train tickets, on receipts from dry cleaners, and on the margins of newspapers. Every blank space, every piece of scrap paper, Mr. Abram covered in tiny, barely legible writing. He also collected the used envelopes from his son's letters, and the larger ones, like the X-ray envelopes they use at the clinic. He would sit on a bench with a bottle of glue and for hours on end, he would glue strips of paper together. Glued together onto paper, they looked like kindergarten cutouts.

"And here I have everything, don't laugh. See, all on index cards. I've gone through A," he'd utter through a cough. "Do you want to see? Abramowicz . . . Appelfeld . . . Aszkenazy . . ."

Mr. Abram carried his notes in a plastic bag from the Internal Export Company, Pewex. He'd begun working on the letter B and ordered me to think about publishing. I haven't seen him for many years. I don't know what happened to his cornucopia of biographies. Out of the ordinary, ordinary and extraordinary. The finished ones and the ones that were abruptly ended. As if Mr. Abram ripped the ticket into two, kept one half of it, and used the other half to light a cigarette.

6

THE PACKAGE FROM Ms. Tecia was very heavy, as if filled with stones and not old photographs. I wasn't even interested in my room anymore, I quickly threw the contents of the wraps on the table and I started to organize them like a game of solitaire.

Of the pre-war photographs, on cardboard or with decorative edges, quite a few, maybe even a few dozen, survived. In any case, definitively more than people. The ones who survived then have already passed away. Their photographic shadows were the only things left of them. Here a small portrait of my grandma in a Hashomer Hatzair uniform, the stamp says atelier Dager on Dzika 3, the year 1925. This is before she met Szymon, and later Jurek—the one with Ms. Pela, who talked her out of going to the Mandate for Palestine—after all, here in Poland so much revolutionary work to do. Then, Aunt Nata, in a blouse with a collar with a rose, still unmarried, "Artistic Photography Studio of Halina Skowronska >>Rafaek<<, Warsaw, Tłomackie 1. Tel. 504-22." And then with Uncle Zorach, in Krasiński Square. Above their heads, cobbler Jan Kilinski is triumphantly waving a saber. The picture was taken in 1938, before they escaped via Vladivostok, Shanghai and Yokohama to America and later to Eretz Israel. Six years of wandering, six spins of the Earth around the Sun to wait through Hitler, who in this time turned their city into a desert of debris. Next, Uncle Szulim, "Photo Djana, ul. Ś-to Jerska 13," that's in our building, on the ground floor, right by the gate. Great grandfather Yeruchim also had his picture taken there. He didn't have to go far, just down the stairs,

35

because my great-grandpa never had time, only a few minutes between his Hebrew lessons, between one page or another of his commentary on Shulchan Aruch, which I have never read, though its title—undoubtedly important, was inscribed next to the titles of half a dozen of other books on my grandpa's tombstone made from a light Jerusalem stone.

Then, the grandmas: one of them on a chain ladder, somewhere near the Zawrat mountain pass, in pantaloons and solid boots with crampons. The picture had an inscription for Grandpa written in soft pencil, March 1939. Maybe it was a trip they took together? Or maybe it was the time they went on a long trip with Mr. Leon and Ms. Pela's Jurek, when they went up into the Red Mountains in the Tatra Range, the last summer before the war? But it was with Grandpa, they carried these photos across a large swath of the world: from Warsaw to Łuck, from Łuck to Kiev, from Kiev to Tashkent. And earlier, they sailed down the Volga River, or the Dniepr, who knows, there is no way to check now. Anyway, it was then that Grandma and Grandpa locked themselves for a moment in a sailors' cabin, and later, already in Uzbekistan, my grandma gave birth to my mom on the floor of a mud hut. That's where my mom had her first picture taken. She is staring curiously into the camera, dressed in a frilled dress of cretonne as if wearing the clothes of a much older sister. The next photo shows the two of them together—my mom is sitting on my grandma's lap, above them a portrait of my grandpa whom both of them would never see again. Because when they were finally allowed to leave Tashkent, my grandpa left his work with Strojbat[2] and went to Sielce, and from there to Lenino, where he was killed by a stray bullet during the Battle of the Brotherhood-of-Arms, second lieutenant in a beautiful uniform, as *beautiful as the Oka river, which like the Vistula, wide and deep, will not wither*[3]. They wrote poems about him and he became a hero though he died right in the beginning. He even had a cargo ship named after him, and when I was a kid, I thought we could

---

2 Strojbat—a workman's squad (from Russian).

3 Fragment from a popular army song. It was composed for the Polish Army that was established in the Soviet Union during World War II.

take it to America, me—my grandpa's grandson—and the sailors saluting on the deck, but I never sailed and the ship was probably scrapped. So, I had to settle on a collection of medals locked in red cases upholstered in plush red fabric, with an eagle pressed on the lid. They were sitting in a cabinet next to the miniature rotunda made of gray plastic that had fitted glass in the middle with a picture of the monument in honor of those who died in the battle of Lenino, a monument that looked like a helmet abandoned in mud. And the only portrait of Grandpa, which he had signed for Grandma when he was going to the front to fight the Germans, enlarged and encased in glass hung above the sideboard in the dining room—so Grandpa could look forward, and my grandma could show him with great pride to all guests, whether they cared about my grandpa's portrait or not.

So, there are no pictures of Grandpa, but there are plenty of pictures of Szymon. Here, my grandma and Szymon stroll down Nalewki Street. There are a few versions of this photograph, as if someone decided to follow the pair on all their dates. There are pictures from the summer of thirty-seven, and from late fall of the same year. Cabs race down the street, you can hear the horses' hooves rhythmically hitting the cobblestones. Young, trimmed trees don't offer shade, so the signs on the storefronts gleam. Umbrella sellers, hat sellers, furniture repair, right behind the gate, third floor. Pudgy advertising columns gleam with their shiny steel-pot helmets, and the crosiers at the top shot into the sky. My grandma and Szymon proudly walk arm in arm in the middle of a trottoir, a toque next to a hat, as a young couple should. Only their outfits change: grandma's white dress from the picture taken in the summer switches to a tight, dark, fall overcoat, and Szymon's loose-fitting jacket turns into a double-breasted topcoat with a wide collar, the kind that nobody wears anymore. Passersby step out of their way, and in one picture, a fat man follows my grandma's petite body with a covetous look.

Szymon is Uncle Szymon, because he never married Grandma, but later they remained good friends. He died when I was still very young, yet I do remember him pretty well. He had

a hoarse voice, and he laughed very loudly when Mr. Leon (and
the two had known each other since their school days) was telling
a new joke. And when he wasn't laughing, he was talking about
politics, that's because at Uncle Motia's on Przyjaciół Avenue,
in general everybody talked about politics as if there were no
other reasonable topics to discuss over an afternoon snack. And
I remember, when Uncle Szymon, who for some reason really
didn't like Edward Gierek[4], was explaining to everybody why
Gierek, who looked like an old effigy yet was featured in the
news every day, should already go to hell, and that the Partisans[5]
(a word, which Uncle Szymon always pronounced with utter
gravity, and so I knew it meant something bad) still have a lot
of influence in the Central Committee, not to mention the
Mokotów Prison on Rakowiecka where there are still plenty of
them and they act with unchecked authority as reactionaries do.
And I really enjoyed these conversations with Uncle Szymon. I
could listen endlessly to the fights between him, grandma, and
Uncle Motia—who is good, who is bad in office, who is a pig
and who's just an idiot, who is getting support from the Ministry
of Internal Affairs, and who, thanks to this, will get a promotion
soon, or who, it seems, may have his party card taken away. And
what does it mean that the *Trybuna Daily* hasn't mentioned it.
Uncle Szymon yelled, and Uncle Motia tried to calm him down
explaining to him why he was wrong. Mr. Leon, if he was present, always sided with Uncle Szymon, and my grandma mostly
sided with Uncle Motia, who would finally be so agitated with
everything that Mr. Leon said (he always spoke so fast, as if there
was a fire!) that he would bring the latest issue of the *Polityka*
magazine for everyone to see what Rakowski wrote about it,
because if *Trybuna* wasn't covering it that was because someone
upstairs gave an order. Then, finally, Ms. Lena would speak,
and then Uncle Marek, who didn't always speak but when he
did speak, could yell even louder than Uncle Szymon. Hence,
I was never bored, and only once, by accident, I pulled off of

---

4 Edward Gierek—the First Secretary of the Polish United Workers' Party in the 1970s.

5 Partisans—nationalistic and anti-semitic wing of the Polish Communist Party.

the table the tablecloth with the whole dinner on it, and a bowl of fried beets landed on Mr. Bialer's pants. I started crying and Ms. Lena was getting upset since a few drops of plum compote fell on her two-piece suit-dress. Thankfully Mr. Bialer wasn't angry and he said that it was no a big deal and there was no need to talk about it anymore, after all, the boy didn't do it on purpose, worse things happen. It's a good thing that Ms. Hanka wasn't there, because, since she didn't like kids, she would get really upset, and like this, Mr. Bialer, whom I liked very much, promised he would one day show me his medals that he got as a guerrilla fighter against the Nazis, and the aunt who was with Uncle Motia right away brought an apple pie, the best in the world. My aunt baked amazing apple pies and in general was the best chef, not like my grandma, who had many talents, but in the kitchen she could even burn matzo brei on low heat.

They only didn't want to talk to me about the time before the war and their loved ones who were lost to the war. But I learned anyway that back then when he dated my grandma, Uncle Szymon lived on Nowolipie, or on Peacock, or Pawia Street, or another street of the Jewish district named after a bird. Somewhere there, one or two blocks away, ever since he was young, he'd worked in his father's woodshop—the place is long gone from the map, bushes grow there, or maybe there is a building made of glass and aluminum. In a picture older than the ones from their walks, because it was taken in July of 1930, he and my grandma stand in front of it: my grandma in a trench coat, and Uncle Szymon in tsyg—industrial cotton pants with his head uncovered because Uncle Szymon was from the kind of house where the young ones, after reading a lot progressive literature, were beginning to ignore a little their religion and the commandments and they would forget to say the Amidah three times a day even though it was an immemorial tradition of every pious Jew. On the other hand, Szymon was scared of his father, who was known as the noble reb Tojwie, for reb Tojwie was very well-respected in the whole northern district, and his family and his woodshop were well-known, and he had regular contractors for his wood. To avoid hurting reb Tojwie's business, his son wouldn't dare to openly break shabbat, so when he had a sudden urge to smoke, he would go far away to a different part of the city.

That picture of Szymon and grandma in front of Tojwie's woodshop was taken clandestinely. The young like each other. Maybe we will need a chuppah? They didn't need it, it so happens, but the picture is still here. On the back, the handwritten note in pencil is almost effaced: "This picture is completely random. Bronka didn't give me this photograph, but I stole it. I don't have any others. Grunia." Did Grunia later give it to Ms. Tecia, her best friend since Free Polish University? And Ms. Tecia packed it into her box? Maybe Uncle Motia or Abrasza—the one who moved to Rostov, stored this photograph? I should have asked, now there is no one left to ask. Too late. Before, it was too early, or I was too young. It's boring with old people. So, unbothered, they took this knowledge with them. Time knows no returns, and the traces of the past scatter quickly, like ash in the wind spreading toward the four corners of the invisible world. Like a token of Grunia, the oldest sister, who was killed leaving two, maybe three photographs behind—the only proof that she had ever existed. From Aunt Grunia—though do I have the right to call her my aunt, since, as it happened, I was never to meet her, and she, when they were killing her, could not know that one day I would appear here connected to her by blood? In one of the pictures (the year 1933) she resembles the philosopher Simone Weil: metal frames on a pointed nose, hair pinned into a bob. In the next picture, taken in a studio and framed, Aunt Grunia is sitting in a masculine tailcoat, a tie tied in a knot, the way a good mathematics teacher would. Is it from Łuck, where they lived with Motia, or is it already from Lviv where everything had its end? The trail ends right after the Germans enter, June 30, 1941. Followed by three days of pogroms in the Jewish districts, when the Nazis and the Banderivtsi[6] chased people and rounded them up, arrests and executions. They wrote about it in books, many saw it with their own eyes, but a picture cannot

---

6 Banderivtsi—Ukrainian nationalistic militia.

be stitched from so many unknowns. Did she die in the street, or did they drag her into a gateway, where it was more convenient to murder? From a German bullet or a Ukrainian whip? Or maybe they executed her the next day, during the massacre in Brygidki? Nobody will ever know the truth about her last moments. A photographer wasn't present there with Aunt Grunia. Thus, I see her only the way I can, like in a silent movie: she's walking or rather running into an unknown Lviv street, in the direction of the train station, maybe her luck will hold and she can catch a train to Łuck, that is if trains in those days of the last judgment are even departing from Lviv. And she is running in a plaid two-piece suit with a satchel where she keeps her grade book or a roll of revolutionary pamphlets. Her heels make clicking sounds against the sidewalk, faster and faster, the bob falls apart as she is running, and the cross-shoulder bag is getting caught in the flying tails of a light summer coat thrown over one shoulder. Grunia is trying to find her way in a crowd of people like her, caught in a trap, dashing in all directions without a chance to escape. The following image is faded as it if were stored on an overexposed film.

There is one more photograph of Uncle Szymon, also in the street, I think it's Kupiecka, because they had erected there a building in the alleyway, it can be checked on pre-war maps, also because it was close to reb Tojwie's woodshop. This is what you can gather from the photograph, but there is no caption. The sidewalk is more crowded than Nalewki: street vendors call out to their clients to visit their booths, drivers maneuver their coal wagons raising waves of dirt, above the stores flap linen awnings. And a smiling Szymon is walking briskly with a bundle of newspapers in his hand, behind him a Yeshiva Bocher, lost in his thoughts, walks proudly in his iron-pressed gaberdine, reading from an open book. In the front, a young gentleman in a suit and a hat and round-shaped glasses on his nose. Where and how did this bespectacled man end up? And the young man in the gaberdine, the kosher butcher, a bearded man sitting on a stoop, an elegant lady wearing a hat decorated by a single feather, a passerby with a plaid scarf, the fat guy with a thick document folder under his arm who cast a covetous glance at my grandma in Nalewki? Our whole Warsaw! Did they do it here, or did they take them to Treblinka? Like with our neighbors on Świętojerska, like with the whole Rabinowicz family who lived on Pańska, the relatives who owned a warehouse with goods right on Targowa, in the front, like Szymon's mother and father, his brother Szlame, two sisters—Ryfka and Malka, cousin Jurek and his wife Hala with their little Herszel, who was supposed to start public school when the war began. Which of them survived, taken in by good people, or because there was not enough room on the train, or for some other unfathomable reason, for example, thanks to an intervention from our indolent Creator, who could no longer tolerate the butchery and decided to act, or due to a failure on the Devil's part, who for fun or, worried about his own wellbeing, left a few souls in the world as a souvenir? Or maybe it was just a coincidence of events that allowed a few to walk out, to bear witness, to scream and lament, to never forget, or to forget forever and yet to remember—from generation to generation, till the end, till the last breath, or maybe even just one day longer.

That's about all that is left from this old world.

7

A glow-in-the-dark evacuation arrow gleamed on a wall in the hallway pointing to the stairs. Obedient, I followed.

Through a crack in the glass doors came a bracing current of night air. A nice change after the stuffiness in the room. I forgot to open the window. The door creaked, so fearing that it might cause even more of a ruckus that would wake up the entire boarding house, I sneaked through the smallest crack possible. Here, the first-floor terrace faced the backyard. A few wicker lawn chairs damaged by sun and wind, a little table also woven, and above it, a slightly dirty parasol of navy blue and white wedges. Like a seaside resort, just that there are only trees and sand here, no water.

Mr. Chaim liked sitting here. In a chair, he would rest his head on an inflated pillow. His eyes lingering on the pine crowns. Mr. Chaim looked ahead and voraciously breathed fresh, resined air.

"Almost like we're in the Land. Why do you think that Jews like this 'line'? It reminds them of home!"

Home. Somewhere faraway. A few days on a ship. The pioneers' settlements in Zion. Tiny houses with red-roof tiling. Rosh Pina with stone porches wrapped in lilac flowers. In the backyards, rhododendrons spread, stone pines pretend to be regular pines. As if somebody transplanted them from Europe. Everywhere palms and citrus groves, then just the sun and the sand. They will start vineyards and they will drink wine, they will grow gardens and their fruit they will eat. The volunteers tasked with drying the wetlands in the Jezreel Valley. From Warsaw, Cracow, Vilnius, and Bialystok. Young guards. Many have died from the pestiferous air. Many have died of the Arab muskets. Many have died from the pestiferous air. Hope is two thousand years old and it is not given to all.

Pine trees. The saddest of trees. Mr. Chaim explained it to me a few years later.

"Each pine is a treasure. Before the war, I donated to Keren Kayemeth. At the end of the month, they would come with a blue tin can to our middle school. Trees for Galilee. The headmaster made faces, he was a serious Bundist, but he did allow them to collect—as long as he didn't see it. He never gave a penny."

The headmaster Rajzman wanted to stay and fight for a better future in Poland. Zion, he explained to Mr. Chaim, is a solution for a small band of teenagers. Masses will not travel there anyway; they deserve a dignified life here where the Vistula River flows. Is there another place for us, a place where a Jew, like a tree, can be transplanted overnight? A poor man, a sick one, an old man? He's put down his roots here for centuries, can you uproot him and order him to yet another exile? We need autonomy for Jews in a common state. A state for the average man— Jew, Pole, or Ukrainian. So, headmaster Rajzman fought for his state, for progress and justice, he edited public responses and wrote fiery articles for the *Folkscajtung*, he organized workman circles and together with his Polish comrades he went to Labor Day demonstrations where he was beaten by the police of the Sanation regime[7].

Mr. Chaim planned to travel—to Palestine. A Jew, a permanent wanderer, is always on the road, and only in his own land can he truly find rest from humiliation. Only when we are home will we lead the life of a free nation. For now, to break away from the shackles of slavery, we have to work very hard, so once we're home we will know how to work even harder. They sought that future during Hachshara, on their own farm somewhere near

---

7 Sanation regime—Polish right-wing government in 1930s.

Warsaw, Mr. Chaim can't even remember anymore where, maybe it was somewhere near Radzymin. They would talk through the night, boys and girls, about this faraway homeland, kibbutzim, new cities including the largest one by the Mediterranean— Tel Aviv, about justice, about the collective and the self-defense squads which will ensure that Jewish life will no longer depend on the mood of the wealthy of this world. They danced hora around the fire, and burning with inner fire, they sang songs that praised their Land. Anu cholkhim, anu baim, yesh avodah, nita etzim al haslaim, gam bahar vegam bagan. We will plant pines in the rocks! On Saturday evenings, their instructor, rosh pluga, Icze Ginzburg, who wanted to be called Icchak Bar Lev, standing by the map would explain to them Palestineography or would tell them stories of chalutzim. And all of them had to prepare a lecture in the still strangely sounding, sitting in the throat, not-yet molded to their thinking, language of their forefathers. And each day except Saturday from dawn to dusk they trained in their occupations. And he, Chaim—the son of a pious craftsman from Brody who only once traveled to Lviv on business and who did not believe in the betterment of the Jewish fate before the day of the Messiah's return, with a song in his heart plowed with a hoe through the Masovian ground, so he would know how to farm his own soil, in the color of ochre.

The war broke before it was Mr. Chaim's turn for bricha— illegal immigration. There was no point in hoping for a British certificate, that would be like waiting for a visa to America or Curaçao. Beleaguered by crowds, the headquarters of the Zionist Coordination for Equality was bursting at the seams, everybody wanted to leave, to escape from Europe as quickly as possible. Too late: as the Germans made progress on the front, the gateways of the continent were closing for refugees like a prison grate that falls under the pressure of its own weight.

Headmaster Rajzman, a Bundist, died in Warsaw, in the ghetto, at least that's what they told Mr. Chaim. Actually, apparently, he died of typhoid before the final solution, in 1941, at least early enough not to be overcome with doubt about his party's program. From his group near Radzymin, Mr. Chaim was the only survivor, totally by accident, or maybe on a whim of God, whom Mr. Chaim no longer knew how to trust after the war. Dead: Motke Fiszman, who knew Hebrew better than others and, making no mistakes with vowels, could recite Bialik's poems; Rojwen Klejman, known as Little Rojwen or just Little, who wanted to settle in Jerusalem, right by David's Citadel, which he used to admire on colorized postcards with British stamps; Szulek from Pabianice, a tailor's son, also skinny and fragile, the youngest in their group, who one time almost got a beating from farmers near Radzymin, but another Chaim, the Big Chaim, rescued him. The Big Chaim, in defiance of his name, also dead; and rosh pluga Icze Ginzburg, an energetic redhead with sparkles in his eyes and who did not have time to truly become Icchak Bar Lev; and rabbi Ciechanowski who used to visit them on Friday evenings and give them Torah lectures on the prophets and who often told them that soon they would be like Jehoshua ben Nun, the successor of Moshe Rabbeinu, and that they would return to the land of their forefathers. The girls also died: Mina Kalisher, tall with thick braids, who looked kindly at the Big Chaim, they even had plans to get married in a few years though rosh pluga Ginzburg explained to them that there was no need to get married in the kibbutz because that's a petty bourgeois relic from galuth; and Dinca Mahler, the daughter of a wealthy merchant from Lviv who preferred their family going to America over Dinca learning how to farm; and Rochl Polaner, a wiggly-giggly girl, who was all over the place and who could play guitar and who kept a yoman, a Hebrew diary, where she recorded in beautiful penmanship dreams and plans—not just her own, but also of the other comrades from her group, all plans that they'd intensely discussed at night in the moonlight. And finally, Rosa, petite Rosa, quiet and serious beyond her age, who squinted her dark blue eyes when she looked at him, and more and more often, he couldn't sleep at night because of her, he dreamed of the days when the two of them would lie on the ground in a kibbutz, embracing between the palm trees or at least on a Polish meadow, right there near Radzymin. Petite

Rosa would let his lips touch her lips—always slightly moist and always slightly parted as if they were awaiting something, and maybe she would even let him unbutton the top button of her shirt, and the next one would give way under the pressure of her heavy breasts and she would show him how much she desired him, and they would be together, and he would feel like he was in paradise. It wouldn't matter anymore if they went somewhere or stayed right here because bliss holds on to the blissful ones; as his grandpa Chaim Mender used to say: the happy know no hour.

The memory of those years that he so desperately tried to get rid of chained him with a heavy chain to this place and, continuously stuck under his eyelids, would not let them close—during the day and even more so at night. The war separated him from Rosa, in any case, perhaps Rosa did not dream about spending her life with him and maybe she had other adolescent plans typical of girls her age, who change their minds and the boy they quietly yearn for. After all, they never lay on grass together, not even near Radzymin, because he was always too shy to ask her, or maybe there was no right occasion. Anyway, Icze Ginzburg always exhorted them to work harder, and Rosa, who was always the first one to fulfill his requests, merely followed him, Chaim, with her eyes, looking at him carefully from behind her thick eyelashes and burning inside a little. In any case, no one knows what would have come of it, probably things would have fallen into place very differently than how he had planned back then, but right after the war, when he came back, he knew for certain that Rosa was gone, that he didn't need to look or check, she was gone and that's it. It wasn't just a feeling, he knew it very well because right before the war, Rosa went back to Hrubieszow, and there no one had a chance to survive. This was told to him by a Polish man with whom for a while he shared the same bunk and a bunch of rotten straw at night, hugging each other because it was terribly cold and they were only wearing their striped, tattered clothes. The man saw all of them goaded along a dirt road. To the nearby meadow. And to the pine forest. Women, children, and old people. Between the pines, they made them dig a ditch, a few meters long, corpse-wide. A dozen or so salvos, there was no need for more. The sun was high then, in the middle of summer, 1942. The first cones fell from the pine trees.

8

BEHIND THE GLASS the silhouette of a hunched man appeared. He didn't look in my direction. The doors squeaked, the knob made a rattling sound. He locked me out on the terrace. Not on purpose, I assume.

I knocked on the glass. Luckily, he didn't venture too far into the hallway. A plaid jacket with leather patches on the elbows: just like Doctor Kahn's. The same penetrating stare from curious, protruding eyes. A bald head with no sign of hair. In front of me, there was Doctor Kahn, or was it Mr. Jakub from the dining room? Beak-nosed old men blend into a single figure. At the end of their lives, Jews come to resemble birds—as if they were seeking to fly away with the last effort of their muscles.

"I'd have locked you out here for the whole night," he explained. "Because I can't sleep, an ailment, you see. Sometimes, before the dawn I manage to shut my eyes, just as others are getting up. Would you mind visiting me in my room for a moment?"

Mr. Jakub. A dear friend of the Director. And an old friend. There are only old friends here. The enemies are also old. Maybe we are too old a people? Even the Lord, he too is very old; he marked a man's age at one hundred and twenty so that no human can compete with him.

"The Director," he continued to perorate, "you know, don't worry. It's a tough post to sit at. It's not his fault that there are no people here, right? He's not to be blamed for this, but it's still his problem, a real Jewish problem, like a loan from a bank. You don't have it—not good. You have it—even worse. And what is the solution here? What is he supposed to do? Knock on heaven's door?"

A black heaven remained shut tight. Stars glimmered amid crowns of pine trees. Early morning moonlight, pierced with thin streaks of semi-matte clouds woven from fine linen, was rising to reveal the trembling and uncertain face of the material world.

He coughed again. He did it in a slightly theatrical manner: a deep cough as if he would cough his lungs out.

"We all have some kind of Jewish problem. I, too, will die soon. And that's it. But you have to suffer a bit longer."

He chuckled. To suffer. About seventy more years and you won't have to worry about any of it. That's what Mr. Leon used to tell me. Seventy years. That's how old Ms. Tecia's photographs were.

"The young," Mr. Jakub's left index finger was pointing at my chest now, "don't care to come here." He shook his head. A nugget of amoeboid-like phlegm flew from above the balustrade right into the courtyard. "But then again, where would we get these young people from? From thin air? For some time now, our people here are only the elders, like back in the time of Methuselah."

Like in Noah's time, just waiting for the flood. History on repeat. One more we won't survive. The beams of our ark are much strained, ribs are cracking, and the holes in the hull are getting bigger, just wait till the last bits of the tar that kept together the ark chip away and a heavy stream of water forces its way inside.

We slowly began to cross the hallway. First turn, another one, another door, and another, a third and fourth. I thought he limped slightly, though he walked briskly into the dining room. Now, suddenly, he seemed to have aged again. At least that was my impression. A semi-stiff hip, like Mr. Bialer's. I wonder if it is also from the days of guerrilla fighting. It seemed he noticed that I was observing him.

"That's nothing," he muttered brusquely. He didn't want to be stared at as he walked.

Another rattle of the lock. Strangely loud in this quiet. Light bursting from the inside. Doctor Kahn always kept all the lights on. And a flashlight on the nightstand. Just in case, who knows what can happen. When they come, at least he will see their faces. Anyhow, sleep, like a whimsical demon, comes rarely, and when it does, it's dressed as a specter. Like the painting in Doctor Kahn's office, painted with the heavy strokes of a wide brush: a skeleton with skin stretched over it, an anatomical specimen placed in full in formaldehyde, following you with the dead stare of its sunken eye sockets from behind the thick glass. But the other painting, the one that wasn't framed, across from this one: a rolling field, actually a smooth, pinkish plank, stumps of crowded dark figures looking like bowling pins. Kind of like the ones I used to play with in kindergarten, but these were brown and black—and we didn't have this kind, just red, green, and yellow. During each visit at Doctor Kahn's, I stared at them, at their rough surface, for a long time, and I imagined that, imperceptibly, through the spaces between colorful spots, I could enter into the painting, and I would be able to walk among the thicket of these human bowling pins, and maybe I could even reach the place where there are just their heads, and even further, beyond the horizon, where I was sure there were more rows, more and more tightly packed, as if the painter wanted to use the space to the fullest and fit in as many as possible. I was only worried that since the represented land was spherical, when I reached the other side, I'd not be able to find my way back. And I knew that no one among the living would be able to help me, because even if the adults gathered in Doctor Kahn's living room paused their conversations and began to worry where I was, it wouldn't occur to anyone to look for me inside the painting, so none of them would be able to rescue me, and I would have nothing else to do but to wander there for the rest of my life. And yet, against all of this, I adored those moments when I could sit on the carpet, with my back resting against the desk, listening to the nicely lowered voices coming from the other room and gaze into the forest of figures staring at me with their nonexistent eyes. Sometimes, the painting shone with a pale light and I thought that I could see a silver glow stretching above the figures, and they reached out of the painting to populate the room, sit comfortably in the armchairs and on the sofa, or insolently squat down on the shelves of bookcases. Then, I would escape from the office, away from the atlases and thick books; I would escape in fear that the doors leading to the hallway could suddenly close and I'd stay trapped, and the mysterious figures from the painting would kidnap me and take me to other rooms in Doctor Kahn's giant apartment, including the rooms I've never been in, full of even scarier, crooked faces in the paintings that were peering out through the dotted glass doors.

"We're here, please come in," the voice of the man in a plaid jacket brought me back. "Here are my quarters!" he stated with pride.

The room I was led into was stuffed with vintage furniture, probably because the owner wasn't satisfied with the standard furnishings provided to the typical guests of boarding houses. Books sat on the table and the windowsill. Not that many: some popular novels, a few thicker books in brown paper covers with their titles written on the spine with a black marker. They were brought here from downstairs, from the ballroom. Even to this day, Mr. Abram's book collection still serves guests here. Detective stories are good for insomnia. In boarding houses like ours, they always keep many of them. Doctor Kahn also had a shelf with detective novels. They were placed in a windowless middle room, right next to a small case filled with strange objects, which on occasion, if I persisted, Doctor Kahn would take out, shake the dust off of, and explain with great patience how they found their way to his house and what they are used for. Treasures from travels, from the peregrinations of Doctor Kahn. Everything was there! A tiny ship with a barometer sunk in the hull to tell the weather, an empty caramel candy can filled with marbles with a name written in a strange alphabet that Uncle Motia or Grandma could read from right to left, a plastic anchor with a "Jaffa" sign and a broken thermometer, a gold-tinted, seven-armed candle holder with a dark stone base, a jar with tinted sand carefully layered into a camel eating in the shade of a palm, and finally, a large shell with an intact pearl where you could always hear the sound of ocean waves breaking against an unknown shore.

"Ma tovu ohalecha," he hummed. Jacob's tents. Why would we have to live in tents? To roam through the desert such unfathomable distances only to find ourselves here where we are?

"Did you find your bed?" He stared at me attentively. A man called Jakub. Every name means something, and they say your entire life is encoded in it. The patriarch Jacob. A heel-catcher. Because of his twin brother's heel that he'd grabbed while still in their mother's womb. Where is your brother, the hairy Esau? His house of straw, ours of fire. The prophets can also be wrong: sometimes a fire can go out if covered with a lot of straw, leaving only a plume of dark smoke.

"Do you know this story from the Bible?" he asked as we were sitting down adjacent to each other at the table. "And, Jacob left Beersheba . . . this is a parshas vayetzei, an autumn section, that was read in the prayer house as the leaves were falling from trees."

He was lost in his own thoughts. Pine tree branches rustled. There was a long pause. From the road we could hear the whirring sounds of the rare passing car.

"I almost don't remember," he rubbed his tired forehead with his fingers. "Vayetzei Jakov miBeerSheba vayelech Charana . . . There was this kid on Łucka Street. He knew the whole Chumash by heart. The whole thing, every letter. Boys would sit him down on a barrel and wouldn't let him off until he finished. And what for? What good did knowing the Five Books of Moses do? Did the Lord listen to him more closely?"

Jacob went into the unknown. To the land of his grandfather, Abraham. May your brother's anger be appeased. Rivka knew what she was doing, she set it all up from the very beginning. The Messiah will leave Israel one day and wipe out the wise sages from Edom. Maternal instinct. Escape from here now, when there is still time, before it's too late. And the Eternal Lord will bless you. Itzhak, a noble and blind father. He didn't understand the story too well. Or maybe he didn't want to understand it? He died content and at an old age. Then, the Lord had benevolent ears.

"Vayfgaa bamakom . . . He lighted upon the place. Discovered! Walked up and found! It was right in front of him, huh? Nothing like this!"

He lifted his hand up. It fluttered like a leaf.

"He collided with the place! Do you know? Do you understand? Why did he crash into it? Nobody understands it, nobody knows, and there is no one to ask!"

Our sages. How many of them we had! All of them sunk in letters. A secret logic unfolds from them. Vilna Gaon could spend whole weeks on a single page of the Talmud. That's how you can save the world—that is if it lets you. And if it doesn't— no book can save it and all books will burn with it. Did Rabbi Shlomo Yitzchaki, a cheerful winemaker from Troyes, know about it? They will sow the fields and grow vines, and collect the fruit of the harvest. Through grammar to the heart of things; nothing is by chance, every mistake in the Torah's text teaches us something if our minds are open enough. And if we close them—no chance for the world to come. No chance of paradise for erudite travelers and peripatetic men under the watchful eye of the Prime Mover. For, the Holy One—Blessed be he, is pure thought. They teach that this is what the greatest of them all claimed: Maimonides, a caustic elder in a round turban who had the audacity to copy the Torah with his own mighty hand. From Moses to Moses, nobody like Moses has come into being among Jews. For two thousand years and then some. It's only been eight hundred years since the second Moses, so we still have to wait for the third one. The Lord has time and he's not known to hurry.

He hung his head.

"There is nobody left to ask," he spoke into the room and his voice echoed against the walls.

"Before the war, you just had to go out in Nalewki Street on a Saturday afternoon when Jews were leaving the prayer house. Everybody wanted to know, to share their thoughts. Like they say, as many people, as many opinions. After all, it is said that a sage can walk ahead of the king. So, everybody wants to be a sage. That's normal. Just that back then, there were so many sages, you could pick and choose as if selecting a ripe plum."

In Beit Midrash, they sit across from each other. They can see each other's faces like in a mirror. Young men searching for the Lord in the letters, or maybe even between the lines. It's easier to

study in pairs, that's what they say, that Shekhinah comes easier
this way. Or, as the saying goes, two heads are better than one.
More noise than in the street—everyone is yelling, everyone
is debating. The tops of the desks squeak, in their hands volumes framed in brown leather, frayed from use, flutter. So that
with their collective strength they can defeat Moses, and if their
strength is sufficient, maybe even God. He enjoys such duels,
they don't seem to cost him much, and after all, nobody likes to
be vulnerable. Why would the Lord enjoy this? Line after line,
slowly, because the syntax of Gemara is so intricate, and it is hard
for a simple Jew to get to the heart of the Law. So, one of them
is reading and the other is checking to see if he missed any vowels, whether inadvertently or from a lack of prudence, or even
worse, because of a sinful spite, he assigned the wrong meaning
to a sentence. It is a matter of great importance, because as we
all know, the devil is in the details, hence the fate of the universe depends on him. They sit and sit, the time is fleeing, and
here every, even the tiniest, word needs your attention, maybe
even for you to hunch over it and nestle it in your arms—as if it
contained a spark from the Holy One, or even just a precursor
of his true name.

"He collided with the place," he repeated with emphasis.
"With the place, and with God himself! Are you surprised? How
can you collide with something that's hollow? With something
that isn't there?"

He stretched. His protruding eyes glistened as he was staring
at me. He will also disappear soon. There always has to be the
last person in the room, somebody who turns the lights off.

"This matter occupied me when I was a young man. I used
to question my teacher, Rabbi Shpicer, Moses Shpicer was his
name. I bothered him every single day of the week and every
Saturday. Rabbi, how is it possible for a man to collide with the
Lord? Because further down it says that the Lord is in this place
yesh Hashem bamakom haze! He told me there was still a lot I
needed to learn. Chumash, then Mishna, later Gemara, the commentary, then the commentary on the commentary, and then
more commentary. And in all of them, not one but a hundred

paths, or maybe even a thousand, and each of them leading to the Almighty. Which one should be taken to reach him? Which one should be taken to reach him on time? Rabbi, which one is good for me?"

He rubbed his burning forehead. The spark hidden in the depth of his protruding eyes began its dance. Very different from the one in the dining room. He bit his ash-colored lips and tightened his grip on the arm of his chair. He began again, slowly.

"Rabbi Shpicer took his time to explain things to me. It took a long time, so long that I no longer remember any of it," he let out a sigh. "Just his hoarse voice, because Rabbi Shpicer had throat problems. I'd recognize this voice anywhere, even in the next world, at least that's what I think, though it's been more than sixty years since we've seen each other, but I know his voice better than I know my, blessed-be-his-soul, father's voice, my father's brothers' voices, my own brothers' voices . . . But I cannot recall a single word! Can you believe it!"

I remember Doctor Khan's voice. Sonorous like a trumpet, and not the least bit hoarse. When he was cleaning my ear. In the office with a strange painting that swirled in front of me as I leaned back, so that Doctor Khan could check my tonsils. And now, together, we will say out loud: "Ja-cob! Ja-cob!" His collection of orange rubber ear pumps. Like an army, or headless dolls, bowling pins from the painting, but this is something you can't play with. If you behave, the doctor will show you how to check blood pressure. A stack of prescriptions bound into a booklet. When I grow up, I'll have the same kind of thing. And once again, "Ja-cob! Ja-cob! A big boy." No other words I recall.

He was quiet for a moment, and then he asked again.

"Did you find your bed? It's made comfortably?"

I nodded. He knows better. He knows where my room is, the one I returned to. The one where they, we, used to stay.

"And our forefather, Jacob, barely had a few stones up there in the desert to rest his head. It's not an easy thing to be a forefather!" He chuckled and turned somber quickly. "The Torah says that when Jacob rested on those stones, he envisioned angels running up a ladder that started on Earth and reached to the heavens. It had to be like those suspended bridges, so that the sun could roll on it from dawn to dusk. At least that's what I think."

He scratched his bald head. Frustrated. A tiny graphic design poster at Doctor Kahn's. It was in the corner, usually covered by the fringe of a curtain. A swarm of winged angles. All of them hitched to flexible rungs of the ladder planted on a solid, rocky land. Not thicker than half a finger, the ladder is shaky, it's actually swirling in the air and it can fall into pieces at any minute. And they, the flesh-colored spirits with translucent faces, are swarming at the top, by the very roof of sapphire clouds, almost brushing the sky with their white flight feathers.

"You're knowledgeable on the subject?" He got curious and then answered himself, "I have no doubt. You remember the old days. Then Jacob woke up. Rabbi Shpicer promised me he would recount Midrash up to this story; he found a new commentary in a book, but I was too busy to see him and listen."

Doctor Kahn and his medical dictionaries. He hunched over them smiling. Papers spread around him and a red apple that he peeled with a thick knife. Like at Uncle Zorach's: a green apple and a ruddy peach on a small plate. Here and there, the serviette had juice stains. There was more than one thing I didn't ask about. Where does influenza come from? Where do the nasty bacteria live, the ones that made me bedridden the winter break when I was supposed to go to Zakopane? Is hard candy really bad for your teeth? And why can the heart never go bust? And if it does, like it did in Uncle Szymon, then why couldn't he get a different one, a replacement, so that poor Uncle Szymon wouldn't have to lie alone in the cemetery, so he could visit Uncle Motia again and get into a fight about politics with Grandma and Mr. Bialer?

"I didn't go, so this counts as my sin," he joked. "I have more than one. But who doesn't sin? You know? For example, let's look at the present time." He stretched comfortably, probably a little amused. "We're sitting here without our heads covered. Sin! Actually, two, because there are two of us. Two sins!" He raised his voice triumphantly. "Did we say the evening prayer?

No. Again, two sins! That brings the total to four. And birkas hamazon after our evening meal? A waste of time to even talk about it! Four and two, that's six. Just one evening. And were our meals kosher? Also, negative! Eating non-kosher is a special sin. So, then? Throughout your life, you collect a whole cart of sins. What am I saying, a cart? A whole train car!"

The sins of the previous generations. What kind of sinner was that boy who was placed on the barrel? The righteous ones, the sages say, God takes faster. So there is less time for them to sin and they are tied with the eternal knot of life sooner. But He gifts sinners with a long life, so that here, on earth, they have time to fix their vile behavior. Such is the Lord's logic and justice.

"A sin is a sin, and that's the Almighty's problem, not mine," he added solemnly. "But I truly regret that I didn't see Rabbi back then. It probably won't be until I reach the next world that I will learn what the deal was with Jacob's son."

He gave me a look. The young comrade understands! He looked around and stopped at the windowsill. As if there lay thick volumes full of the wisdom of previous generations. Inside them, rugged pages, and outside, damaged covers hanging on them like old clothes.

He stretched his dry lips—two lines drawn across the face. I wanted to reach for the carafe of water, but his hand stopped me. Do not move now. He was silent for a moment, as if he were gathering strength. He arched his neck and his eyes froze staring at the ceiling. I followed them. We stared at a striped shadow of the lamp. Not more than a few minutes passed, but it seemed like an eternity. Should I go now? This may upset him. Should I stay? You never know with the elderly. But then he spoke. This means: I stay a little longer.

"I won't forget the day Rabbi Shpicer took me to his library. It was on a Saturday, and we went there right after a dinner at his place, before the afternoon lesson, when we were repeating sections from Rashi. Just the two of us. It was a great honor, because Rabbi Shpicer didn't take boys from my cheder to his library. He didn't let anyone in, because he was worried that they would take his books. So, I followed him and I knew that I had to inspect everything minutely and memorize it all, so I could tell the boys and they would believe that I really saw our teacher's books. Because if I were to miss something, one of them could say I was lying. And how could I be sure I was the only one from the entire cheder that Rabbi Shpicer took to his library? I was very worried, for what if he took all students there and then asked each one not to tell the others? Who would know his ways? It was a large room, huge, and in it, thousands and thousands of books! The room was packed with them—on the shelves, on the windowsills, on the table, under it, on the chairs. Even by the radiators. And Rabbi Shpicer seemed so tiny! He maneuvered between them like an acrobat so as not to step on anything. He pulled some out and put them on the side, he returned others, and it was obvious that he remembered very well each one's place. He didn't even need to check the titles. He recognized them by their weight, size, the type of leather used on the cover. If his eyes were covered, he'd still know what to do. He ran around for about half an hour, and I observed him as if somebody put a spell on me! I felt dizzy, but I couldn't move, my legs felt heavy."

He pointed to the water. I poured from the carafe. He emptied his glass in one gulp.

"I'd thought that Rabbi Shpicer took me there to discuss whatever the parsha was for the week that had just passed. That it would be the same as in the classroom, when he listened and then explained with patience. But this time, nothing like this happened! I just stood there and stood there, staring at the books, each (I was deeply convinced) Rabbi Shpicer had read cover to cover; not only that, he knew them by heart and was able to recite them from memory. And I was all alone there, because not only did he not pause even once to look at me, he didn't even say a word to me, he just muttered under his breath, and I had no clue what questions I could pose. And in a tiny voice I said to myself, Great Lord, how much do I need to know to make you proud and for Rabbi Shpicer to pass me to the next grade?

Because if Rabbi Shpicer, a teacher in our tiny cheder, had read all of these books, how many books does one need to read to become the head of the Yeshiva? How many to be a good Jew?"

Woefully, he opened his arms. As if he had just returned from Moses Shpicer's library.

"The Lord didn't answer me then," he smiled sourly. "He's still not providing answers, so I don't know. And Rabbi Shpicer? We went back to the classroom because the end of Saturday was approaching. And all the boys looked at me, jealous that it was me and not them who went to the library. I worried that they would ask me questions, because if I saw our Rabbi Shpicer's library, now I should know answers to all kinds of questions. I was tongue-tied. I didn't know anything! And I started to cry, and I cried through the night. I remember it to this day."

9

A FOG SAT above the trees, wrapping the area in a cold touch of invisible drops. Its lower, heavier billows shimmered, veiling the light from sodium lamps like balls of cotton candy on sticks in different colors. The wind snuck around almost listlessly, not causing much trouble. Only clumps of dry juniper sagged slightly, inviting a longer walk.

Świdermajer houses[8] were soaked in the night. Only here and there, between pines, a delicate light emerged, infiltrating with great effort the cover of twilight. Wall studs and purlins, veranda windows, zinc-tinted gutters and front porches with planters, misshapen chimneys—all remained in a state of sleep, unavailable, separated from the street by a fence of shrubs, stalks, and rampant weeds.

A boarding house called the "Ray of Light," a rather impressive edifice composed of irregular boxes of different sizes, with red letters above the door, like the words on the boxes of chocolates from the Wedel factory. Villa "Felicjanka," or actually "-e-janka," because the simple modernist "F" and "lic" remained only in the form of scars scratched on the entrance gate. And over there, among maples and wild acacias, there is probably the "Ark." The sign faded, but it's easy to recognize it by the two concrete posts flanking the entrance to an overgrown garden. The place has changed, immensely. A small, two-story, wooden house—the wood painted yellow, green, and beetroot red with a

---

8 Świdermajer house—typical of the area, wooden summer houses.

veranda downstairs and a teeny balcony upstairs. A flat tar roof, and empty spaces for windows. It had sunk into the ground like a rotten root. A stone pond lined with moss, the path around it, or whatever is left of it—heavy stones stuck in the sandy ground, between them rows of unkempt greenery. Inside, planes of paint chipping off from the ceiling like stalactites.

Further on, a steep dune begins. An embankment of sand, permanently tousled by winds that exposed twisted roots. Or maybe these were the limbs of some creature that burrowed in the ground and had passed away? But I don't know anything about this, because it simply didn't occur to me back then that someone could die and lie there, as if nothing had happened, covered in sand from the dunes. Maybe I thought about dinosaurs that went extinct before we came into being? Most likely nothing of this sort, we, Mr. Leon and I, simply came here to look for the best tree bark to make new boats. Mr. Leon stood in the sand up to his knees and cut off large pieces using a knife he'd brought from the dining room, because he didn't want to use his pocketknife in case it got nicked on a hard tree knot. Then he clambered back onto the path, short of breath, helping himself along with his hands, both dirty from resin, and as he was shaking the sand off of his pants, or just from his socks, banging his moccasins against each other on the path with dust flying off in all directions and birds lifting off from branches in a panicked flight, he cursed under his breath in Russian so I wouldn't understand. Then we would walk back home, proud of our treasures, and our walk took forever because Mr. Leon was telling me how he had to collect wood in the winter in the Siberian taiga for fire, and when he was telling me about it, of course he had to pause to point to something in the sky with his finger or to draw with a stick on the ground, so he would lose most of the pieces of bark, and we would have to go back to the dunes, because Mr. Leon didn't want to do any damage to our garden, anxious that the Director would get mad or that Mr. Abram would find him and ask in a stern voice what right Mr. Leon had to trample on our communal garden. It was quiet, only gravel crunched under the soles of shoes. In this stillness, a dog began barking faraway. One, then another, then a third one, and so forth, all just waiting for a signal from the first. Their baying echoed through the woods, from the neighborhood with boarding houses to the train tracks, undeterred by the wire fences. I was always afraid of dogs, the outdoor dogs, and the scary gray-fawn female German shepherd that prowled the rooms of Uncle Szymon's apartment indifferent to the guests gathered in the living room. I remember a pack of dogs roaming here right behind the gate of the boarding house and near the forester's lodge where we stayed if rooms in the boarding house were booked. First you had to walk down a sandy alley, if I recall correctly, one or two turns, then across heather fields and then across hazel groves. The same groves where, one time, Doctor Kaminska took me for a walk and we got so terribly lost that we were almost late for dinner because Doctor Kaminska didn't know how to find her way in the woods. Only after an hour of walking in circles and clawing through the shrubbery did a local man in a plaid peaked cap tell us we were walking in the wrong direction entirely, and then he had to lead us to the place where the paths forked and even I knew how to get back home. Back then, the forest was much bigger than today, now it's just a few paces wide. Or maybe the groves were before the fields—because in order to reach the heather fields, you had to cut through a long clearing with a high-voltage line where a transformer, locked in a brick tower, hummed. The forester's lodge was much further, behind the transformer, which I think was at the mid-point. Anyway, it just seemed that if you reached the transformer, everything else was very near, even the tiny meadows where I picked mushrooms that I then took to the cook, so she could make a soup, but she immediately threw them all away.

In fact, we didn't venture too far into the woods, because the prettiest spots were right near the boarding house. Later, when I was older, I was allowed to go out into the road on the other side of the fence. It had to be a very sunny day when they took a picture of me as I was entering our garden's side gate, the one near which I later found a dead pigeon. I was getting ready for the road and pulling behind me my wooden toy train that moved like the real ones until it got derailed on some jutting stone and the wheels of the locomotive fell off, and even the man working in the boiler room wasn't able to nail them back on. But before this catastrophe, I walked pulling my train far away behind the corner, and later everyone asked me how far I had gone and only Mr. Leon looked sour and said that a train isn't an airplane or a ship, and then he repeated again that, when I grew up, I should be an engineer who builds machines, or a great inventor, because that's the best way to serve humanity.

So, a long time ago I took walks here. I have a photo where I'm sitting with my legs spread over a bent pine. The tree should be somewhere near. Just a few steps. In the picture I sit where the trunk bends, and I'm in an autumn jacket and a balaclava though it's the middle of the summer. Now, in the fall, a few years later, I won't find this tree—every other tree is bent; I won't recognize the voices of that forest. It seems that all my actions here are an archaeology of a memory sunk in twilight, like trees and bits of wooden houses. It's easier to spot a faint shadow of what's passed than the dawn of a new life. Mr. Abram read it to me from some book. Or maybe it was from the notes he made on scrap paper? Or maybe it was a transcript of his journal, because Mr. Abram kept a proper journal, but apparently he asked for it to be destroyed when he was already very sick, because he didn't want anyone to read it. Individual pages sat on the table in his room, next to bottles filled with pills and a metal box with needles. Under the red stained glass of Josef's tribe. A fertile strand of vine arched over a pond that will never go dry. It will propagate and they will be like Efraim and Menashe. And they will bless future generations every Saturday. But not us.

Mr. Leon, Mr. Abram, Grandma, Ms. Tecia. Branded by what happened and that—the moment they left—collapsed into nothingness again. Their lives and mine, among shadows, amidst specters and among ghosts that substituted for rays of sunlight. Instead a bitter taste of passing. And too many reminders of old age? Too many meds, coughs, and memories of those who are no longer here. Those who were killed during the war. Those who died later, or left or scattered around the world. A melancholic landscape. That's how it has to be. Probably, it's opposite to what those who brought me into this world and who had the ambition to guide me would have wished for me. Nothing ever turns out as planned. The clever wit of Mr. Abram as he argued with Mr. Leon about the revolution. Everything always ends badly. Or maybe they didn't want it at all? It just happened this way, a random circumstance, and it's no fault of theirs. Someone else decided this. Nor were their grandparents responsible for preparing such a future for their grandchildren. But earlier, long ago, it was natural that people came into this world and marched forward, toward life, and passed away when their time came. And then things have changed. Or maybe that's just the impression we get and every previous generation was similar to this one in their insistent will to survive and their defeat?

On the other hand, those were also happy times. There was a lot of laughter, and you can't say that anything foreshadowed the end. Did I think about it at all when my mom and I ran around the garden counting toadstools in the green grass? And when we were running away from Ms. Hanka, who sat in her beach chair and complained that we were bothering her again and that she didn't go on holiday to have to deal with children in her old age. My mom wore a hat made from folded pages of the *Warsaw Life Daily*, and this got under Ms. Hanka's skin as she argued that my mom destroyed a paper that otherwise other people could still read. And when we used to borrow cards from Mr. Chaim, so we could play War on a bench on the terrace or on our room's balcony if it were raining and it was not possible to take walks in the woods. But also when we took walks with Mr. Leon in the Łazienki Park and he got it into his head that we had to find a frog house, or a basement where King Stanislav August had kept frogs, so he could eat them for dinner. Mr. Leon, as usual, was arguing with Grandma, and there was another man with them in an American cap with a visor. And this man gave me a stick of chewing gum. As he grew tired talking with Grandma about Gierek and the latest changes in the political bureau, Mr. Leon told me a story about kings and their chefs. I don't think the story was very compelling because I remember that my legs started to hurt from walking in circles, because Mr. Leon kept promising me that he'd recall in a moment where this awful frog house was, and when we finally found it, there were no frogs there, just broken garden rakes on top of a pile of slightly rotten leaves. Mr. Leon was deeply disappointed, the man in an American hat, who was on a brief visit to Warsaw, made fun of Mr. Leon saying that he was confusing a child, and Mr. Leon was greatly offended and gave the other man a few sharp words in an unknown language. The man responded but soon enough everybody laughed, though Mr. Leon, still upset, was grinding his teeth. And they had another heated debate about politics.

The most important thing is that I can still see them standing in the alley by the palm tree hothouse smiling to one another. Grandma, Mr. Leon, and the other man, whose name I don't know or even where he came from, and I will never know this. The same is true with my mom, she's standing on the path to the forester's lodge that I couldn't find now, but which I know for sure existed at the edges of our wonderland, in this magical place where the train tracks turned and the land was becoming slightly damp and from which it was impossible to go any further because it seemed that all paths lead to nowhere and the surrounding wall of the green forest didn't really exist but instead was painted on some great magical curtain that reached from earth to heaven.

I picked up the pace. Trees were getting more sparse. The train tracks should be somewhere near, maybe ahead of me. The spine of the line. It's safer along the tracks. The green light of a semaphore blinked friendly from far away. This means I'm close to the station. I learned how to count here. I'd spent hours watching the train cars roll through. There were more of them than in the "Locomotive" poem by Julian Tuwim, because *there were forty in a row, if I recall, what did they haul, and our line*—sometimes we had a hundred. They slowly emerged from around the corner, different shapes, the ones with large double silos to transport cement were the most interesting. And the very long ones with wooden logs. And the cargo ones, gray-black or brown, bolted. At the time, I didn't think I disliked *sicher* bolted cattle cars.

The tin bells of the boom barrier began to tinkle, signaling an approaching train. The last suburban train to Warsaw, or maybe a night train to Lublin? Depends on the direction it will come from. The Lublin-bound train doesn't stop here, we're not important enough. The rumble of the train was coming from the Warsaw direction. Lublin-bound. From the darkness, still far away, a triangle of bright yellow lamps emerged. I always enjoyed this view. Who is traveling and where? What concerns are calling them? Or maybe this is a ghost train, entirely empty, rushing in an unknown direction and without ever intending to stop? This one was coming fast. Our station wasn't included in the schedule. The siren gave a long single blast before passing. A string of cars passed in front of me, a row of bright windows flickering like a filmstrip. I couldn't see any passengers—maybe it really was empty? Onward it went. The racket of train wheels, deafening for a moment, was fading quickly, and only the two red lights of the last car still flickered through the thickness of the woods.

I crossed the gate. The sharp edge of its silhouette separated the illuminated boarding house from the thick brew of the night. A very strange edifice. I could never draw it in my head from memory, the way you can with regular houses composed of an entrance, walls, windows, a roof and chimney. Ours was designed based on various geometric figures, according to the rule of functionality. The big-city simplicity conjured up a multitude of shapes and right angles, subordinating the rhythmic façade.

That's what they say. But I know that it always looked out of place here, though the place knows many curiosities. Long and languid like a caterpillar and slightly spilling over. To walk around it was a real adventure—you had to pass all the porches, stairs leading up and down to the darkest basements that were not open to the public, and the engine room of the mysterious ship that our house would become during heavy rains, the water flooding the captain's bridge and wide waves crashing against the portholes of the cabins on the passengers' deck. In those moments, we sat inside listening carefully to the roar of the storm and the rattle of the downpour, and it seemed that any minute we would break the chains that were still holding us in place, and the speed of the gales would kidnap us and, chased faster and faster, we would fly away on the backs of the long-maned clouds. And we would glide like this all night, and maybe even into the next day, until we would disappear in the vast vortex, only the lighted chandeliers in the ballroom marking our place on the bottom of the ocean.

10

THE LIGHT SEEPED from behind the dining-room doors. The Director and Ms. Mala sat at the table. She in a quilted pink bathrobe, he in his daytime outfit. They looked like two wax dolls attached to their chairs. An iron teapot was heated up on a portable electric burner. In front of them sat a Parcheesi game with tokens in perfect rows. It didn't seem like they had started to play yet.

When I entered, they simultaneously turned their heads toward me.

"Oh, it's you, sir!" The Director called in a friendly manner. "Please, please! Night owl! Please sit down, there is enough room," he encouraged.

"With pleasure," I thanked him, though not being sure why. Again, I wouldn't get a chance to see the mural in the ballroom.

They pulled an extra chair closer.

"A night owl," he repeated. "Everybody here suffers from insomnia, it's typical of boarding houses," he looked around. His empty house and his Jewish problem.

"I'm sure the coal man is asleep at this hour," Ms. Mala noted.

"Asleep, asleep," he teased her. "It's a good thing that he's asleep! What would you prefer, ma'am? That he was getting cozy with the waitress?"

"How dare you!" she pretended to protest.

"That's right." Proud of himself, he banged his hand against the table. We continued to sit there for no reason. With a waitress, it would be more fun. A young, local girl from next door.

She probably went somewhere with the coal man, her kind does not stay here for the night. More likely in one of the wooden huts that I was passing—dark outside, but inside life carries on.

Two pairs of eyes stared ahead from the wall. I didn't notice them here before. Not him in a gold vest and with his hair styled in soft curls and with a hat rakishly sitting on the top of his head; or her, more visible in a red dress with a necklace of precious stones on her open décolletage. Their countenances strangely absentminded, as if it were not true that they enjoyed each other's company, as if the painter caught them in the midst of some intimate conversation. A Jewish fiancée. That's what they call her, but they keep quiet about him, they don't call him fiancée. What they do tell is that they were called Isaac and Rebekah, and they lived back when Spinoza was writing his treatises. I used to take them for Shylock and Jessica. He, a helpless and jealous father, holds in his arms a fleeing Jewish child. She, in a moment, will slip away into the big wide world.

"And one time," the Director began again. "A girl who used to work here captured one guest's heart. Do you remember this, ma'am?" he asked her, looking for confirmation.

The old woman did not respond.

"Nooo," he was surprised. "His name was Rubin. From Szczecin. Actually, from Łuck. He wasn't young, yet he completely fell head over heels, do you understand?"

Proud, he raised his hands up like some kind of impresario advertising his pupils' performance.

"I can imagine," I tried to quiet him down. But it only made him more energetic.

"Everyone told him, 'Mr. Rubin, what do you need this for? For the girl is young, she's not interested in you in the least. Is this appropriate? She could be your grandchild.' But Rubin would respond, 'But what am I doing? I'm just looking. Who said that it's forbidden? I'm still alive! The Lord hasn't taken my eyes away yet! If he wants, he will take them away and then I will not be able to see, but for now he doesn't wish it! He wants me to see!' And if nothing else, he'd go with her to the kitchen and he would want to help set the plates. He gave her gifts, gave orders to buy her perfumes with the dollars that he got from the the "Joint" for being a veteran. Ah, I'm telling you, he lost his mind completely."

Ms. Mala looked with disapproval.

"He always pokes his nose into other people's business! How is it your concern that he lost his mind?"

"Concern? Fiddlesticks!" He became irritated. "I'm just entertaining the guests. How is that your business?"

"And you were doing what? Stargazing when she was serving dinner," she giggled.

"Meh, you're such a know-it-all! What could you know back then, ma'am? Even a horse would laugh."

"And, you, sir, are a donkey." she said, offended.

"Nonsense!" He turned his back to her. "You know," he began again privately, "the Rubin guy, he walked back and forth, he lost his whole pension. He was saying he'd take her to Israel, but all she would answer was, 'Mr. Rubin, stop following me!' But she took both, the perfumes and the dress he bought her. And then she did go, but not with Rubin and not to Israel!"

"You should have let it go by now!" Ms. Mala lost her patience. "Better you should bring something to serve with the tea, Director." She emphatically stressed the last word.

"Fine, fine. There is no fire." He seemed slightly embarrassed. "Whatever you need."

"And so, tea." he ordered. The kitchen window remained shut.

"Service, darn it," he cursed under his breath. "You have to do everything yourself. The king without his men," he gave a false laugh. "Like a brothel without . . ." He shuffled his feet to drown out the last word.

"What did you say?" She was curious. "Has anyone seen a king here?"

"Hah!" he mumbled and disappeared in the backroom.

As soon as his steps faded, Ms. Mala gave me a look.

"We're breaking the rules a little by sitting here. The Director orders everyone to go to bed and meanwhile we'll sit here drinking tea. And he is extra nervous today."

"It was a tough day," I noted politely.

"A tough day. Humid." She shook her head and looked around.

"And he's an old hothead. Even the coal man can't stand him."

All of them are old hotheads. Mr. Leon yelling at the night guard because the latter fell behind in one of his tasks. A loud and quarrelsome world of uncles and aunts. Everywhere tumult and hum and endless conversations over cookies and coffee. As if they had nothing else to do, and that with their pointless chatter they wanted to model again the form of the best of worlds. I almost don't hear their words anymore, I don't recognize voices in the dark, stirred into a single stream pulsating inside my head. But what if I can't remember their names, can't recognize the faces that I can barely see and that sometimes seem like a sketch of a single countenance, a trace of one and the same mask.

From the next room we could hear a clatter of dishes. A metal object, a pot lid, rolled with a bang onto the floor, rattling a moment unpleasantly until it froze.

"What the Devil!" The Director's voice trembled, he was in a really bad mood now.

"Is everything fine? Has something happened?" Ms. Mala worried.

A wooden counter creaked. The Director peaked out from behind the kitchen window.

"Nothing, nothing," he calmed her down and disappeared.

A moment later, he appeared in the door with three ceramic cups, a box of tea, and a box of biscuits.

"All's fine."

He placed the cups symmetrically, added tea, and poured hot water.

"See, like in a proper hotel," he praised himself, and a big smile appeared on his face. Soon, though, his facial expression changed. He banged his hand against his forehead.

"Damn it, I forgot to bring sugar."

"Don't worry about it, we will sugar the tea on pridumku," she consoled him. "Like in Russia."

Constant stories about Russia. And about wartime poverty

in Uzbekistan, where tea with sugar was drunk three ways. On prikusku, where everybody licked the same sugar cube dipped in a pot of hot chai. On prigliadky, when the sugar cube was too small to be felt on your lips, so it was better to stare at it placed in the middle of the table. And when even that was not available, you would sweeten on pridmuku. The third approach was the one that Grandma and Grandpa used most often. They brought from Russia a passion for samovars, though no one back then on the banks of the Syr Darya River thought about samovars. Later, the samovars sat in the living rooms: brass, squat, unused. Ours was heated by coal, Uncle Motia's—electric. A memory from the old days, from the motherland of the proletariat and from Tashkent, the city of bread and rotten apricots, which Grandma picked by the roadside when nobody was looking. All those stories about extreme poverty when I refused to finish dinner. A time-tested moral blackmail. A good overcoat exchanged for a tin can of sour milk. And mini-bagels on a string, bubliczki, hard as a stone, which Grandma somehow got for my mom and which somehow fell on a stone floor and crumbled so badly there was nothing to pick up.

The Director sighed and dipped his lips in the tea. He slurped it for a moment. Then he fixed his eyes on me again, like he did back in his office.

"Did you find your room?" he double-checked.

"Yes, up on the first floor," I confirmed.

He didn't want to leave me alone.

"So, did you find your bed? Did you visit your old grounds? I remember you. You sat with us at our table. Nagged us with your questions."

"I said right away that he would find it. They lived up there; I remember well," Ms. Mala came to my rescue.

"I remember nothing," groaned the Director. He grimaced, scratched his head, and said sarcastically:

"Probably Jakub took you there? He knows every corner here. Our guide.

He didn't tire you?"

"Not at all."

"He was probably telling you about his Rabbi, right? An old raconteur. Everyone here has a story like this to tell. A giant sale of memories, like in a Jerusalem shuk. And each story like a patterned carpet, just that they are giving it away for free, because nobody wants to buy."

"Better, you tell us something," the old lady requested.

"The old days," he grunted rudely. "What is there to say?"

"So, let it be about the old days," she agreed.

"Fine," he said kindly. "Let me show you something."

He got up and walked toward his office. He came back so fast that we didn't even have time to exchange glances. He was laden with a stack of old books and newspapers. He threw all of them on the table between the cups with tea.

"Once in a while I come across some old papers," he said, as if he were trying to explain himself.

"Here, this is a phonebook. One guest from America brought it for me. Just our neighborhood. Five hundred numbers, and how many Jews? Four hundred."

Ms. Mala and I leaned over. A tiny book. Not like the register of phone owners in the Warsaw network. It held so many names! One time I dialed our number, the one on Świętojerska. 12-09-28. The metallic voice of an automated service tried to convince me this number does not exist. Other ones, the later ones, also do not respond. Or somebody else lives there. Grandma's scrawls. A notebook full of old numbers. Crossed out one after the other. Not active. But a notebook also can't be thrown away, after all it might be useful. It lingers in a drawer.

"It's worthless in today's world," the Director announced, closing the covers. "But you've collected, so you're holding on."

I nodded. Another collector. In this building, everybody collects something and gathers it up for eternity. Mr. Chaim's collection of broken light bulbs—they might come in handy, the rummage at Doctor Kahn's, Ms. Tecia's grand collection of postcards with stamps from all over the world. Voices were coming from afar, and I no longer knew who was speaking: the Director or them, back then. Actually, the Director.

"Oh, see?" he soliloquized, showing her the next book.

"Please, look here. Huh? Where would you like to travel? We have the largest selection of health resorts: gastro hyper acidity and a prolonged lithiasis of the bile duct that leads to the inflammation of the mucosa, arthritis—for this we have Urazin, citric-salicylic piperazine also helps in cases of lithiasis, but is equally effective with arthritis. Diabetes mellitus, Maria's Springs, Szczawnica, Krynica, ah, ma'am, if you only knew, those were the days!"

He fell into a reverie. A grand director of a medical facility. He missed his vocation. I can see him in white scrubs as he is ordering his patients to take walks around the/a spring with palm trees in a health resort. A paradise for Dr. Kahn who adored health resorts and sent everyone there to drink nasty water from tiny porcelain pots with long spouts. Good for the heart and good for the liver. And just the right microclimate for the supposedly sickly child. Oh, here, a purulent inflammation? Thick or watery discharge? Stick your tongue out now. Say, aaah! Don't bite on the tongue depressor. That's right. Upper respiratory tract infection, bronchitic inflammations of the mucous membrane, spasmodic cough due to allergies, tests are necessary . . .

And this one, he will order us to go to Sochi and we will walk up and down the promenade in straw hats, like my grandmother used to and as today retirees walk the promenade in Tel Aviv from Jaffa to the yacht port. Better yet, if they all stay here, with him. Because everybody here will eventually find his or her place and time.

"Ah, if you only knew!" he half-closed his eyes.

Our doctor. The one who used to take visits here, his name was Lewin. He specialized in the respiratory tract. And, the other doctor, Doctor Centnerszwer, practiced in the area of surgery. We had therapeutic sulphuric mud baths, sodium chloride-rich mineral water, showers with a jet nozzle and adjustable pressure. Physiotherapy, Sollux lamps, individual and group exercise sessions. A tennis court and a cricket ground. And in the winter, an ice rink and a sled track. A perfect place to treat neurosis.

"A buildup in the bronchi," the Director was restless. He rested his head on his fists, dug his elbows deeply into the edge of the table, and read in a monotonous voice as if the memory of the world of sanatorium illnesses could soothe his own pains. "Exudation. Bronchitis asthmatica or a prolonged inflammation of the mucus membrane that leads to flaring of the bronchus and asthmatic complications, pulmonary emphysema and death due to central cardiac and respiratory system arrest. See, here!" Delighted, he raised the book up to make his demonstration more compelling for his two listeners. "We're home. Pine tree forests, dry places with porous soil, protected from the wind, plenty of sunlight where the patient can breathe in a natural environment and gain the benefit of the resined air that soothes spastic changes. Volumen pulmonum auctum, a small thing, an increase in the capacity of a lung, usually just one, but the medical establishment knows cases of increases in both lungs always preserving the optimal efficiency of the tissue. It may lead to pulmonary emphysema if not caught in time. In cases of tissue amytonia, careful and individually designed exercising of the respiratory tract is advised. Climate based treatment in places located not too high (up to 500 meters). And then the senile pulmonary emphysema, a very unpleasant condition, atrophy of the lung tissue, irreversible, a general expression of reversing processes. Treatment in old age is helpless."

Like with Grandma and with Mr. Abram. Yet, they began so well. A photo of a young girl with a black dog is still here. In the background a brick boarding house near Warsaw with walls plastered in white and stairs that lead to an entrance framed with wood flower planters. The twenties, no doubt, a stamp in the back, "Photo-Rawicki, (. . .), Zamenhof St.". Here, "on the line". But it would not be possible to identify the place. The addresses have changed. Try to find a photo studio now! And a trace of Doctor Lewin. What happened to him?

"You're not old enough to remember," Ms. Mala pointed out astutely.

I twitched. The Director fumed with anger.

"I'm telling you about the history, and it's still not good enough for you. They repeat the story of the crossing of the Red Sea over and over, and yet no one really knows what happened."

He flipped through a few pages. His own little medical bible. "Oh, and there is also this!" He murmured contentedly. "Those inflicted with atherosclerosis of the circle of Willis fare best in the forested or upland areas, elevations without any dramatic changes allowing for longer walks on an even plane."

"Eh, provocateur," Ms. Mala didn't let him aggravate her. "What use do I have for you teaching me this now?"

"Forget it, then!"

He slammed the book shut. Miffed. Nobody wants to listen to him. He stopped by the door to his office and gave us a long somber look.

"We've almost ceased to exist, and both of you think still—more!"

"Sir, what are you talking about now?" Ms. Mala was surprised.

"No, no, nothing important, just stuff," he got upset.

"That a man can be squeezed out like a lemon and then be thrown away. Ma'am, don't you know?" He added with resentment.

"You can make a compote from a lemon." Now she wanted to drag out the conversation. "The flavor always stays. My mother . . ."

The Director, who was not Doctor Lewin, waved his hand as if he wanted to ward her off.

"Meh, I'm talking about serious matters, and you go on about compote."

He covered his eyes and remained in this position for a while not letting us leave. Finally, without taking his hand off of his face, he whispered,

"They, the wise-men, reckon that a man is made out of a single sheet of bronze, ostensibly, like some kind of golem. That the surface is unspoiled, not a single crack, not the tiniest scratch. And inside him, everything is impressed upon it like against a slab of wet clay. All these centuries from Abraham and Sarah! Enough!"

He went to his room. The dining room went dark again.

Ms. Mala didn't speak afterwards.

Then, I fell asleep.

11

THE FOG, BLUE and thick, was getting denser. It was like jelly completely filling out a giant glass dish. The day was melting with the night, or maybe there was no day or night there, but a primordial mixture of elements, lighting up from the inside whirled billowy clouds over the chasm of the garden.

We sat inside. The time dragged on and lazily stretched, at once moving onward and then freezing, and in those moments it seemed that life froze with it.

That summer, the TV in the common room was broken again, and the viscera of a cylindrical kinescope barely gurgled with gray magma. A sleepy mood enveloped shaded rooms, escaping through the keyholes into the hallways of the first floor, and from there above, to the inaccessible terraces where furry moths were napping stuck to the edges in the cracks of the wall.

Older residents cursed then, what has this world come to? Ms. Hana, who suffered from rheumatism, would ask Doctor Kahn to proscribe her new medication even though strong gusts outside made it impossible to pick it. They canceled the upcoming lectures because nobody would manage to come in this rain and wind. Doctor Kahn had a small disagreement with Doctor Kaminska, and Mr. Leon relentlessly played with the knobs of an old radio to hear the latest weather report. Then he would go to the office with a written request for the management to take into account the advanced age of the vacationer as well as the fact that a significant portion of his holiday stay took place during a predictable meteorological catastrophe and to consider returning at least a portion of the fresh air tax paid by the above. Next, he'd spend hours discussing the results of his futile negotiations with Grandma, Mr. Abram, or Ms. Tecia. Only Mr. Chaim exhaled calmly over a book, flipping through pages but now and then his head would inertly fall to his chest, and then mysterious murmurs would come from the inside of it as if something were tossing and turning, but unable to escape.

Back in those days of confusion, everybody was very engaged, each preoccupied with matters that under no circumstance could be postponed, they would all go to their own corner of the house, run in circles up and down, or vice versa—they would motionlessly sit in their tiny armchairs in the common room, awaiting a change in the weather and listening to Mr. Leon's reports on what was going on back in the big city. It seemed strange because the city seemed so distant, rooted in a different reality, it didn't occupy the mind, which was focused on things much closer and more tangible, things with which we have become one. Those other places were ceasing to exist, they continued only in the memory of those gathered here, just like the squares, streets, and houses that were spoken about during afternoon snack at Uncle Motia's, their names were recalled with solemnity from the depths of a dream past.

No one paid attention to me. The only thing for me to do was to stare, alone, out the large windows of the dining room, behind which a mass of yet-unformed matter evanesced into a luminous pale blue-pink. This fog was at once dropping and rising, and its milky tongues were dancing in space. Drops of water rang in the gutters or squatted on the lightning rods, swollen and heavy. Puddles of mud reached the stairs of the terrace: the sky and the ground floated there among the bubbles growing from shaded slush that over and over swelled as if trying to spit something out of its cavernous insides only to immediately after, apparently backtracking from its original intention and with a few smacks of its lips, close up its throat leaving only faint circles.

During those foggy days, I would meet Mr. Abram and Mr. Leon in the garden where the two relentlessly carried on their own conversations and would tell me about the beginnings of the

Universe. One taller than the other, both very old, they would sit on a bench right by the porch. They would place me between them and begin spinning stories that I could listen to to no end. And it never bothered me when Mr. Leon repeated once more the same story about the philosopher, Baruch Spinoza, who had proven that God is just a superstition of the ancient Rabbis. Or that Mr. Abram, no matter what, wouldn't agree with him, pointing out that Mr. Leon knows nothing about philosophy. In those moments, nothing was important, the world around us would fade, nobody was calling me and no worry could disturb my inner joy. I shivered from excitement, catching their words and arranging them in front of me the way you arrange blocks of a magic square, and they surrendered to my powers then with an ease and simplicity that they never did later.

Bereshit bara Elohim . . . Mr. Abram spoke in a language I didn't know. How does it go? . . . et hashamayim veet haaretz. In the beginning God created the heavens and the earth. The rest can be deduced. I liked the word "deduced," I repeated it aloud again and again, slapping my tongue against my teeth. In the meantime, Mr. Abram continued to patiently describe the following stages of the divine act of creation. As he spoke, it seemed to me that flakes of invisible snow were dancing around his head. He resembled a sparrow that, carried by a gale, would perch on the edge of the bench for a moment of peace. I would freeze, anxious that my slightest wince might cause him to flee before explaining how the Lord dealt with all his work. But Mr. Abram wouldn't scare away so easily, he continued his story, and our garden, empty thus far, would grow green, shooting up with colorful flower petals and serrated leaves of ferns; it was filling up with the juicy scent of grass and the sickening bitterness of juniper. And things I couldn't see before were appearing around us as if they were becoming visible only thanks to Mr. Abram's stories.

Hours were passing, though slower than usually, and in front of us paraded animals and sea creatures of all kinds that God created during our conversation. But, instead of looking at these miracles, I looked at Mr. Abram's face, his ears sticking out like cabbage leaves, wrinkled eyelids that almost spilled over his eyes the color of faded almonds, and cheeks ploughed with a net of red vessels through which life was fleeing. And I followed the movement of his lips turning blue as he was uttering all the words of his story—as if old Mr. Abram alone was to suffice for the entirety of creation. And I waited in suspense to see if he would manage to tell it to the end, before a drop of white saliva would gather in the corner of his mouth to slide down to the ground, and exhausted Mr. Abram would get up from the bench and walk away.

But he wasn't walking away; instead he would start a story of how God came up with the idea of molding Adam, the first man, from clay. He lived in a beautiful garden where exotic trees grew and their magnificent fruit sprang. Adam could pick them whenever he wished because they were always there, and the sun shined incessantly, not like here. And when I'd ask why we don't live there anymore, after all, how could a man be doing poorly in a garden that God made just for him, Mr. Abram would add quietly, making sure that Mr. Leon didn't happen to catch it, that Adam and his wife once picked a fruit they were forbidden to eat, and God grew angry at them and ordered them to live somewhere else.

I didn't like at all this cruel God who chased Adam out of his garden. Because if that were true, then it was possible that one day He would chase us out and where will we go then? So, I'd stop paying attention to Mr. Abram and would turn toward Mr. Leon who was waiting for this moment: God made a man! A wretched blind man, a nice story! He pulled his bushy eyebrows and looked at me sternly, and I, though I usually wanted to laugh when I'd see Mr. Leon, I was afraid to talk to him when he spoke about God with such a forbidding expression. God made a man ... But who created God? You don't know? I didn't know. I think Mr. Abram also didn't know because if he did know, I'm sure he would know how to explain it to me and he'd start his story from the beginning, that is from the moment God was created who then created the sky and the earth, trees, flowers, animals, and finally Adam and his wife. I also don't know, Mr. Leon sounded delighted then. I don't know because God doesn't exist! At first,

I didn't understand it, so I asked my mentor: Rebe, where did God come from, was there something before? Another God, bigger than ours?

I listened to Mr. Leon, and I imagined another, larger God who made the God who made the sky and the earth. He made him from clay the way ours made the first man from clay. But who created the big God? An even bigger and more powerful God? But was he the first one, or maybe there was an infinite succession of Gods lined up one after the other, and each ancestor was stronger and more powerful than the one after him?

When I was asking my questions, Mr. Abram didn't speak, and Mr. Leon just waved his hand, disgruntled. Because Mr. Leon didn't like saying good things about God, that's because back when he asked about Him, his teacher in the cheder, reb Pinchus Menchem, got so mad that he kicked the young Mr. Leon out of his class and then Mr. Leon's father beat him to a pulp for sinning and bringing disgrace upon their pious home. For a few more years, Mr. Leon contested God, because it was important to him to somehow explain God, but when his father caught him with a book by Spinoza, he beat him with a stick and kicked him out to the curb, so Mr. Leon decided that in his case, God didn't act honorably. Because, although Mr. Leon devoted so much time to thinking about the divine Creator, God was mute and didn't even move his finger to protect Mr. Leon. This is how Mr. Leon decided he was mad at God. But when I met Mr. Leon, for some time already he hadn't like Spinoza either, and claimed that we should believe in scientists who long ago explained how the world was created and proved beyond doubt that there is no God in it.

Mr. Abram stayed silent as excited Mr. Leon was beginning his lecture on the stars. In front of me, on the bench, he spread the pages of the paper and with a soft pencil drew dots, circles, and lines that ran in different directions intersecting at times, and other at times running parallel to form impenetrable hieroglyphs, full of sweeping zigzags and knots and loops. From afar, they resembled the rough warts that decorated Mr. Leon's pale face. Here is our planetary system—he punched the middle of the page and expanded with pride, probably thinking that the creation of the world was also his merit. I was trying to decipher those learned scribbles and sometimes I even thought that in the medley of lines I found the bright spot of our sun and a few globules of planets moving around it along their oval orbits. But the picture was quickly getting blurry, and the celestial bodies and their trajectories drawn by Mr. Leon with so much expertise were disappearing between the lines of text, getting lost there and extinguishing like burned-out cinders. Unfazed, Mr. Leon continued his lesson. He arranged nuts and wild apples on the ground and connected them with sticks to form the constellations of Ursa Major and Ursa Minor. Next to them, immediately he was arranging others: the constellation of Cassiopeia from five handsome cones and extensive Orion, who shined in a circle of overripe rowanberries. And before I'd even notice, the garden would become a sky that was the background for comets and meteors made from cherry stones and bits of yarn that rushed onward among nebulas of clover. Spheres of dandelion seed heads generously sprinkled stardust, and the cosmic wind carried this universe's finest particles all the way to the heaps of withered leaves by the fences, to the edges of the galaxy.

Back in those days, the Universe invited us in, so together with Mr. Leon we visited its furthest corners, nestling once and again on some cooler star to catch our breath. And late at night, armed with a telescope that Mr. Leon expertly put together from a paper storage tube, we would sit on one of the upper balconies to observe the miracles of nature. And nothing could frighten us, not even the sight of all the planets of our solar system as they were forming a single row, which was supposed to be a harbinger—as people said on Earth, of incomparable catastrophes and calamities eclipsing those that had already taken place. At that moment, we were like the learned men in Mr. Leon's story, who were able to predict from the smallest flicker of rocks in the sky the direction of events in the entire cosmos, and possibly even to identify the moment when its end will come.

See, we don't need any God for us to know everything! Mr. Leon was as excited as a child. Did Sputniks find God in the sky, did Gagarin see him? No! And apparently it's the best spot to view him from! The best! Because he hides on Earth, so cleverly that the best minds cannot find him. Not even through the electron microscope! He laughed out loud and started again, that in the beginning there was a hot sphere of matter that was expanding to a prodigious size, so that we could all fit in it—me, Grandma, Mr. Abram, and Mr. Leon. And the other ones, those who lived far away from us, in other cities or a long time ago in a galaxy far away. And the creatures that will appear at the edges of the cosmos, long after we're gone, when our Earth will cease to exist along with what was created here.

I stared into the dark of the sky, it spread up close in front of me, and I'd ask Mr. Leon: Is there something behind it? Another sky? And then another one? Or, what does it mean that the universe is everlasting, and that it doesn't have a beginning or an end? I couldn't understand all the words he was using and I felt that I was getting dizzy from everything he was saying. The infinity of the eternal, material universe, which Mr. Leon described with such awe, was as inconceivable as Mr. Abram's stories about the Lord were. Frightened, I knew that I would never completely understand them.

Sometimes, when they spoke about God and the world, Mr. Leon looked angrily at Mr. Abram, and Mr. Abram grew so tense that a knot of veins popped out on his forehead.

They looked like a sparrow and a jackdaw. A conversation about the beginnings of the world would direct their thoughts toward completely different, much darker matters. In those moments, they would forget I was there, and sensing tension between them, I understood that all these issues mattered to them more than you could gather from the jokes that were woven into their tirades. As if their stories—about trees, birds, and stars brightening the firmament of the night sky—had another layer that was hidden from me. They suspended everything between their words, in the diluted, mute air.

And when the fog was falling, again they grabbed my hands and we'd walk across the garden. Me in the middle, they on the outside, wrapped in autumn overcoats. And Mr. Abram's cane tapped the spongy ground and clods of dirt flew in all directions. And so we walked like this from the terrace to the edge of the garden, to the train tracks, where early on, I remember, blackberry shrubs used to grow. And Mr. Abram made me name plants in the garden. I could recognize them by the shape of their leaves, but Mr. Abram told me to invent a name for each that only the three of us would know. No one else, not even Grandma or Ms. Tecia. Secret names for flowers and mushrooms. And if we forget one of them or if we die and we won't remember anything, nobody will decipher their true sound and they will end up in a repertory of forgotten names sharing the fate of the names that were given long before us.

So I walked down the alleys and named each pine and heather twig. I'm not sure if I was coming up with the names or rather finding them there, covered by the ground, between clusters of grass dropped there in advance, many years before our walks. And then I watched at the dawn, as the sun rose, when its first rays were faintly touching the crowns of pine trees, as the garden filled with names, filled up to its edge, to the furthest ridges, and then expanded and took over the whole, unknown to me, world. And in front of the boarding house, between the porch and the train station, a crowd of aunts and uncles stands. Among them dozens of Mr. Leons, Mr. Abrams, Doctor Kahn's doppelgängers, rows of Grandma's girl friends, cousins of Grandpa and Uncle Motia and all the sisters of Mrs. Cukerman. They are standing there and staring at me while the day is still melting into the night, on the edge of twilight, which spills above the chasm in dark waves.

12

A RAY OF LIGHT, weaving between the bars of the headboard, traveled toward legs wrapped in a russet blanket. It went further, past a stool with a basin and traveling items that I had spread by the wall right after I got here, reaching beyond the edge of the door. Light entered the room covering traces of the last hours, weeks, maybe even whole years, as if the night had lasted much longer than it usually does.

I lay still, staring at the brown damp patch on the ceiling and waiting for the monotonous shuffling of wire rakes to rouse me from the remnants of sleep. Behind the house, individual birds were trilling. They called to one another for an extended period of time then went quiet. Maybe they were getting ready for their departure before the approaching winter. A train went by, again it didn't stop. Our tiny, forgotten station with its scratched train schedule board. At the end of spring, we'd get off here overloaded with suitcases and bundles—a plaid traveling bag with my toys and dark blue weekender bag with a hot plate, an electric coil, a dozen thermoses, and then we dragged all of this along a sanded alley. It was supposed to suffice for a few months until the first chilly days, like the one right now, when the leaves in the garden began to lose their Kelly green. We planned to leave as soon as they arrived, because the winter was coming. There was no spring or fall at the boarding house. At least I don't remember them. Everything took place enclosed in the height of summer or the peak of winter. The rest was covered by a fog. A fog so thick you could cut it with a knife. At least that's how Mr. Leon described it.

I stood by the window, at a safe distance from the glass behind the folds of a curtain. Just in case someone—a random passerby or a visitor—would want to carefully inspect the façade, looking for evidence of life hidden behind it. In a delicate aura, I could see from afar a local gardener who was sweeping aside cones in the alleys. He performed the task with gravity, filled with internal dignity and peace. Old and hunched, leaning on the rake, he reminded me of Mr. Jakub. He methodically collected everything and formed small, even mounds as if the cones could be useful to someone. Not once did he look in my direction. Repeatedly, he moved away and came closer, sometimes he looked at the sky, then he'd stare back at the alley. He wore a long white coat that was covering his shoes, more like the kind that pharmacists wear, a rather unusual garment for a gardener. The coat's whiteness was alarmingly distinctive against the greenery. As if an otherworldly bright bird formed only out of a down that lets sunlight through flew among the junipers for a moment. I knew that he appeared here by accident, because he lost his way, and that as soon as he looked around a bit, he'd fly away with a flutter, carried by the first gusts of wind.

There was no one else in the garden except him, nobody was looking at me. And yet, I could feel that right next door, behind the wall, they were hiding. I knew they were not asleep, but they lived in hiding, they were squatting in a wardrobe behind clothes, or in a broom closet, and squeezed into a corner there, they were trying to breathe as quietly as possible. Like Doctor Kahn at his home, hidden behind a satin curtain. I ran around the room listening to my aunt and Grandma yelling "hot-cold" and pretended I didn't see his brown Oxfords. And Doctor Kahn liked to hide a lot, and I think he believed that he was pretty skilled at it, so I poked around under the desk and behind the china cupboard, ignoring all their hints so as to not spoil the fun we all had and to take as much time as possible to discover him. And I remember Doctor Kahn would get bored a little in

the corner, finally stepping out and measuring me with feigned
severity so that I would flee from him deep into a grim labyrinth
of rooms, forgetting that soon the shadows from the painting
would approach me and tempt me to stay with them in their
land of silence.

I wanted to hear the rattle of the blinds and the grating sound
of the windows opening that would give me hope that my neighbors dropped their vigilance and were willing to be seen stepping
out on one of the balconies. But nothing of this sort took place,
though I waited till noon while savoring the sight of pine trees
rustling in the wind.

Nobody walked in, the garden was empty, the windows were
shut. Maybe everyone was hiding in the dining room or the
common room, like back in the day, coalescing around a broken
TV, under the mural of Jewish history? Maybe I should look for
them there? And if not there, where?

Back then, it was easy, because the bustle filled the hallways
from pale dawn. Long before breakfast, even before they managed to burn the oatmeal, doors banged, steps rumbled, the wood
floors squeaked everywhere in the house. Mr. Abram and Mr.
Chaim stepped out in front of the building for a morning smoke.
Ms. Hanka complained that her bones were aching and in her
shrill voice proceeded to tell Grandma about her sleepless night.
Ms. Tecia went to get the newspaper. And in a skimpy swim robe,
Mr. Leon, holding a striped towel, giant toothbrush, and a cup
for brushing his teeth, ran to the bathroom to take in peace his
healing Siberian shower of freezing water. Later, he and Doctor
Kahn did their morning exercising routine. One, two, one, two!
Doctor Kahn waved his arms providing the tempo. Three, four!
In return, Mr. Leon's old back crackled. Five forward bends, five
backbends, two half-squats, a few neck twists left and right. One,
two, three, four, five!

The boarding house was filling up with their shouts, it grew
and brightened because the daylight was entering from all sides.
People were gathering in small circles by the stairs, or on the
mezzanine floor, to have vibrant conversations. Then they dis-
persed and formed new groups until they reached the ground

floor where you could sit comfortably in maroon chairs and wait
for the dining room to open. Behind the door, there was a joyous
clanging of plates. Through a slit, I could watch them setting up
silver soda siphons, the waitresses walking into the room with
soup tureens and platters of cottage cheese with chives. I enjoyed
these moments when we all sat down under the portraits of the
classical Yiddish writers and began our breakfast. Our family
of adopted uncles and aunts, a family different from the ones
immortalized in group portraits. But I don't have a single photo
of Mr. Leon and Mr. Abram. I'm not even sure if I could pick
them out if they suddenly appeared in front of me.

Not much more I recall. At times, almost nothing. My past
sits in me deeply, but when I try to reach it, I encounter a void,
as if I were born yesterday, and everything that happened before
was just a thicket of shadowy images, brittled and scattered into
the grains of atoms that Mr. Leon told me about. The multitude
of these images creates an illusion of memory similar to how a
throng of images can become a substitute for life. I follow them,
I look for them in the dust between cobblestones, on a familiar street, and in the floor cracks. Maybe weakened particles of
the old time—both intoxicating and foul like the scent of gum
arabic preserved in the nooks and crannies of a drawer—have
survived the destruction somewhere? And today I know it is from
there, this dining room where I get the unvarying sense of living
on an island, of inadequacy, of feeling like an outsider. And a
pessimistic sense that everything passes, is old and deprived of
opportunities to continue, is condemned to turn feral, to degen-
erate, and to be covered with a gray frost—can be traced back to
that time when I observed Doctor Kaminska and Mr. Chaim as
they struggled to take small steps at the edge of the forest alley.

Now, when I was passing the row of doors in a hallway, they
stood tall, one after the other, like male nurses before going to
war, and their fronts shone with durable layers of oil paint. But
the plaques with numbers were missing, although they had been
there when I passed by in the evening, and the draft came from
a half-open door on the upstairs terrace, and where I met Mr.
Jakub and where Mr. Chaim had resided, and in the summer if

the weather allowed, Doctor Kahn had played chess with Mr. Abram.

The breakfast hour passed a while ago. Maybe dinnertime? Did they eat without me? Nobody rang the bell. I didn't ring it either. I'm not a child anymore. The last privilege of the young ones, who are all absent now. But has anyone stayed here? Mr. Jakub? And the Director. There is no clicking of his typewriter, which means he isn't in his office yet. At times he resembles Mr. Abram and his journal, especially when he writes out receipts in his tiny handwriting. Our brave recorder. He sits alone and scribbles, organizes index cards, arranges reports, he will leave behind a stack of useless papers. Isn't one of the stained-glass portraits hanging in the corner of his office? Light blue Benjamin, a ravenous wolf, a favorite of the Eternal. He rests safely with him, and he protects him for all days.

The silence in the hallway was broken by a groan. When I came closer, voices from the dining room echoed in the staircase. Surely, the Director went back to the group to end his disagreement with Mr. Jakub. Our historic disagreement, which we have continued since the times of Moses and maybe even since Adam. Like Mr. Abram with Mr. Leon. And Mr. Chaim, who always explained both sides of each case. And he prolonged his conversations about exile from Egypt and about those who stayed in Warsaw. Who stayed and who left. We always depart to never return, but the difference is that if back then no one left, we wouldn't be here anymore. I could never grasp this dark, ruthless logic; for years I was troubled by the inevitability of this choice. Would we not be somewhere else, if not here, then there? If not today, then . . . Because molecules, whose dance Mr. Leon described with such detail, wouldn't they form into our bodies and brains—even if my Grandpa and Grandma had not left the city after the first bombings in September?

I crossed the dining room. It was empty. Nothing has changed. Behind five veranda windows white pillars continued to support the roof, colorful flowers sprang from concrete planters, between the pavement shoots of yarrow grew. Inside, the staff table was still placed under the painting of the Jewish couple. It had been cleaned, but for some breadcrumbs on the plastic tablecloth and three round spots marking the place where we had left our night-tea cups. Further down, behind the glass door, the ball-room spread out. I pushed them. They didn't yield. Both door-knobs were tied with a string. However, I thought I could hear a conversation inside. A conversation I didn't remember or one I wasn't able to hear before. But I could only catch the rustle of voices, vague, blurry outlines of sentences, single words.

My face glued to the crystal glass.

13

WHAT IS THIS fog?! You can cut it with a knife! Where was it designed?

Mr. Leon. His grumblings. They probably spent all morning playing cards with Mr. Abram; as usual, Mr. Leon lost, and later he was the only one who dared to go outside.

"It's a torrential rain," he proclaimed with passion.

"End of the world! For sure, simply the end," Mr. Abram teased him instantly.

"There was a beginning, there has to be an end," Mr. Leon refuted him. "Why is this so strange?"

"I don't find it surprising sir, I'm just worried about you."

"Why is that?" Mr. Leon was filled with indignation. "Why are you worried?"

"What has gotten to him?!" He turned to those gathered.

"The end of the world, and are you, sir, prepared for it? A pious Jew ought to prepare every day for the coming of the Messiah," Mr. Abram explained learnedly.

Mr. Abram always enjoyed elaborating on what is accepted among Jews as custom. To tell stories about our tradition. About the way things were in the past, how people carried themselves, how they slept, ate, and sang all morning in the prayer house. What life looked like back then. How we—how they—used to live. That's something I didn't understand, why this was before and is not now. What happened so that they no longer follow accepted Jewish customs, and for what reason, instead of talking about it to no end, they don't live the way they say they used to live?

Regarding Mr. Leon, that was understandable, because Mr. Leon was a revolutionary, like Grandma, Grandpa, Uncle Motia, Mr. Bialer, and others; and as a revolutionary, he believed in a better world and he spent time in jail for this better world. A new, better world, he explained, has to be built on the ruins of the old one. But, of course Mr. Abram was not progressive, at least not as progressive as Mr. Leon and Mr. Bialer. And I sensed without a doubt that he had a secret that he was hiding from me, something bad, something that prevented him from clearly explaining what was going on with all this tradition and why, as a matter of fact, we don't live the way we did before. Because there was no doubt that Mr. Abram was homesick for the old world, but he didn't know how to turn back time in order to return that world to us. Actually, maybe all of them missed it, but because of this revolution, this materialism, this progress, nobody wanted to admit it?

"And the Messiah! Right in time. What do we need a Messiah here for? They say: how to recognize a false one—by the fact that he has come," Mr. Leon snickered.

Then he added in a more serious voice:

"After all, how will this poor shed accommodate him? Won't we feel ashamed to welcome him here?"

He spread his hands. He lowered his head and looked at himself, then his eyes traveled toward Mr. Abram and further on toward Mr. Chaim, who was snoozing in his velvet chair, tightly wrapped in a plaid blanket.

Mr. Abram decided to cheer up his old companion:

"We'll have a fourth for a game of bridge. Not enough for a minyan," he smiled.

"Not enough, not enough!" Mr. Leon shouted. "But who said that quantity must mean quality?"

"And you, sir, are the one to ask?" mockingly needled Mr. Abram.

Mr. Leon recognized that he went too far.

"You confused me!" he squawked, hurt. "Of course, it means quality—how could it be any other way?"

Sullen, he circled the common room twice. He paused near a kneeling figure.

"Did you see?" he asked daringly.

The Director was plugging up crevices in tall windows. He didn't notice him.

"Gosh darn it! Everything's broken here. Not one nail is straight in this house."

"Didn't you see?" Mr. Leon was not about to leave him alone.

The head of the holiday house flinched as if a bee sat on his nose.

"Did I see what? I didn't see anything and I won't see anything. Dear Lord, just give me a warm corner and leave me there, so I could have some peace. And no arguments!"

"Arguments are our specialty," Mr. Abram observed. "Did we not argue in the desert? The whole time, not a moment's break! This is bad, that is bad, the food is not tasty, the neighbors are bad, cousins not the way they should be."

Back then, it was worthwhile to have arguments. We were only at the beginning of the journey. And now, when we were getting close to the end? How do you fight after this? Does it even make sense anymore? Or, maybe Mr. Abram and Mr. Leon were the last in our march? The last arguers from back there. Their stories full of a vigor and internal strength that they didn't know how to pass on to us because they used them all up for their own survival, for a relentless holding on to life. Their traces are left on dunes, among junipers, pines, rowan trees, on cobblestones and underneath them, between clods of dirt.

"There you go!" Mr. Leon wasn't giving up and cast provoking looks to Mr. Abram. "And so, you won't tell me what you may want?"

The Director tried not to pay attention to him. In silence, he meticulously arranged rolls of blankets in the crevices near the floor. Against his efforts, the fog was still sneaking inside.

"Terrible summer we have this year," he proclaimed.

"Has he ever said that some summer is not terrible?" Ms. Tecia responded from her corner.

"Before the war, he claimed that before the war," Mrs. Grynsztajn explained.

"I don't believe he was here before the war . . ." Ms. Mala wondered. "How could he have been? After all, he's too young."

The Director gave a quiet bark as if he sought to speak up on his own behalf but he immediately abandoned this plan.

"What the devil does it matter? Was here, was not. Not here, then somewhere else."

"A Jewish optimist," Mr. Chaim added. "Tell me, sir, when will it get better? When? It already was!"

"An old joke," judged Ms. Tecia. "For him, it was never better. Director, am I right?"

"Neigh," an indifferent whinnying rose from the lower level.

"Exactly," Mr. Chaim summed up. "Our Director, like Moshe Rabbenu, guides us through tough times, feeds us, gives us drink. Alone he pleads our case with the Lord."

A painting in an album at Doctor Kahn's. Moses argues with God. Two tremendous bearded old men. The Creator's silhouette is straight, his hands are raised in a gesture of reprimand. Moses, Moses! While Moses is slightly hunched, supporting himself with a gnarled stick, this is before he had his tablets that the Lord gave him on Mount Sinai, so we would all know thou shalt not kill. He scowls. Distrustful. Here I am. Could God designate someone else? Perhaps there could be a substitute? And what if I refuse? Will this anger God and will he send one or even three storms with lighting, and then he will leave us in peace and let us go? So some other nation will become the holy people.

Or maybe the whole story would go in a different direction? And we wouldn't sit here, in the common room, the last ones. Mr. Chaim, Doctor Kahn, and Mr. Abram. Also, Ms. Tecia and Grandma would tell different stories and sing different songs. Likewise, nobody would have to flee from the tsar to America and from the Nazis to Uzbekistan. And maybe Aunt Grunia would not die in Lviv and Grandpa would not fall in the war

against Fascism. Only Mr. Leon and Mr. Bialer would probably still want to trigger their revolution and they would argue
with the Lord, if not our Jewish one, then with another one,
and against their fathers' wishes, would not sit at table for the
Friday evening dinner. Or, maybe none of this would come to
their minds?

"I'm not disagreeing," the Director suggested. He stuffed
back-up blankets under the window and got up, stretching his
back and knees. "Who am I to disagree? I drudge here from
sunrise to sunset and then the second shift, from sunset to sunrise . . ."

So, here I am. Hallowing thy name. Like those before me
and the ones who will come after me, if they come. Because,
how many Jews came out of Egypt? One in three! And the rest?
The rest were lost. That's what Mr. Chaim told me—always and
everywhere the minority of us survived. Mr. Chaim would snap
his fingers. He could do it simultaneously with his right and left
hand; he promised to one day teach me this trick. They dissolved
like a sugar cube in a pot of tea. Or maybe it's better for them?
That they didn't experience the yoke of God's curse and lived to
see their old age and were content with their days? Evidently,
somewhere their kids and the grandkids of their grandchildren's
grandchildren live, by now more than a hundred generations, or
maybe even more, and they live in good health and happiness,
enjoying sweet years and getting sad when hunger strikes them,
and they populate the earth with their numerous offspring, as
the Lord promised to Abraham when he was persuading him to
leave his house.

"An exaggeration." Mr. Abram ostentatiously dragged his
hand on the top of the card table and then raised his dirty palm.
"A Jewish exaggeration. Is he also keeping the floor clean with
his spit and polish?"

The Director pretended he didn't hear him.

". . . When would I find the time to chat with God?" He felt
sorry for himself. "Here we go, look at him: he created the world
and now he sits back and watches. Admit it, six days—that's not
a big effort. What is this supposed to be? That's his whole work?

Each and every poor Jewish man would want to work this much. Our Lord is like Meyer Rothschild. Long ago he opened a bank and now others have to multiply his wealth."

"Exploitation! Religion does support an exploitation of the working masses," Mr. Leon pulled out from his memory one of the old slogans.

"Eh. What does he know?" Mr. Abram flinched, "Labor, labor! Did a pious Jew even have time to work? Let's look at a Jewish week, for example. Thursday."

"Why Thursday?" the Director clung to Thursday like it was his last lifesaver.

"'Cause I like it," Mr. Abram was not in a mood to have verbal spats. "'Cause today is Thursday, is it not?"

"Yeah, right!" Mr. Abram expressed his indignation, but he continued to pay attention. The Director just sighed with pity.

"Right, then, Thursday. Prayers of atonement. And a Torah portion transcribed for the coming Saturday."

"Here we go again! Again religiosity—who needs it today?" Mr. Leon groaned. "And who can answer my question?" he stamped his heel.

"Give him a break, sir." The Director grew curious about Mr. Abram's list. "Parshat hashavua? What is it? How much time do you need to read it?"

"A whole life!" Mr. Chaim instructed solemnly.

"Doesn't matter how long; still too long," interjected Mr. Leon. "Science already provided an answer."

Nobody paid attention to him. Mr. Abram winked at Mr. Chaim. They had it coming. He feigned surprise.

"One whole day is too much? Especially because right after Thursday comes Friday. And on Friday every Jew awaits Saturday. What am I saying! He awaits it from the end of the previous Saturday. No other way but the minute he catches the scent from Besamim, he hopes for the next one. He can already see the candles his wife lights in the window."

Mr. Leon twitched nervously. Let me spoil his game. Why is his supposed to be on top? He pulled his chair closer to Mr. Abram.

"And when he's still an unmarried man? Or, if his wife passed away?"

Mr. Abram continued undeterred.

"But Friday is a special day, when he awaits with his whole heart, then the angels come down to earth."

"And capture those willing to go with them to heaven," Mr. Leon finished the sentence.

"No! No! He got it all wrong. Not these angels."

Mr. Leon gave a scornful pout. Mr. Abram turned his back to him.

"Then there is Saturday. Saturday is a busy time. Evening meal, prayer house, dinner."

"Shabes shlof." Mr. Leon closed his eyes ostentatiously. To show everybody how much he doesn't care about Mr. Abram's lecture. Mr. Leon didn't believe in Shabbat or in the seven days of creation described in the Torah and in the books about the history of Jews.

However, Mr. Abram continued. During his lectures, no one could stop him.

"Sunday and Monday, those are days right after Saturday. How can you get down to work? Tuesday, the first day after resting, also a day, as they say, that is a mere transition. Before it even begins, it has already passed. There remains Wednesday!" he finished triumphantly.

Mr. Leon shook his head in disapproval.

"A man barely catches a breath, and already he has to go and pray."

"We're still six days away from Wednesday?" the Director double-checked.

Mr. Leon tapped his head.

"Is he really trying to become a pious man in his old age?" Ms. Tecia's question, asked in a theatrical whisper, hung, like a provocation, unpleasantly in the air.

Pious! How many times have I heard it? A word spoken in a strange tone with a touch of derision yet also with a note of melancholy. Pious and progressive, like an inseparable pair. They were pious, he, Bronka's father, the whole time was hunched over books, very pious folks, but there was poverty and the place was dirty, let me tell you, ma'am, how were they supposed to clean when he was praying and reading all the time, how do you support a family from this? On the other hand, Moshe was the progressive one. On the Judgment Day, he went to the prayer house with a ham. His father said to his mother: My son is dead to me, I no longer have a son.

The Director craned his neck. What do they want to expatiate about today? Get in verbal spats with God? What for? What bother is he to them, if he's not here, and possibly even never was here?

"Pious?" he repeated the question. "What does it mean? Are we sure it doesn't bear some mockery of a devout man? Of a Pintele Yid with a pure heart?"

Ms. Tecia was quiet. Others also decided to remain silent. The Director and his monologues. His right, maybe even his duty.

"Pious," he wondered. "I lost it somewhere along the way. Actually, my father lost it, a wise, devout Pintele yid, the kind who followed in his father and grandfather's footsteps on the path of justice, and yet he lost it . . ."

He took a look at their faces.

"All of us have lost it. That's the truth. They. And we with them."

After the war it seems like we all were progressive and nonbelievers, it just happened that way, because even Mr. Abram, the same Mr. Abram, who once during some argument was called by Mr. Bialer a reactionary, not even he attended the prayer house anymore. So, when I was a kid, at the end of December, we would put up in the dining room a tree with an ornament on the top and colorful glass baubles. In honor of the first star[9], so that I could get gifts like my friends at whose houses on the Eve of this Star, the Christian God was born and they sang ceremonial songs. And only Grandma's brothers in Jerusalem and their sons, and Mrs. Grynsztajn's niece were still devout and

---

9 *Trans. Note.* In Poland and other neighboring countries, Christmas begins on the evening of December 24th. It is customary for the celebrations to start with the first star in the sky. Kids then receive small gifts and a dinner of twelve dishes is served.

did everything the same way as the fathers of the Director, Mr. Leon, Mr. Chaim . . .

Mr. Chaim hissed from underneath the blanket.

"A belief in revolution. The undoing of all Jews. Out of spite for Bronstein, Trotsky ordered the synagogues to be burned down. As if the tsar had not ordered the same. It took a Jew to really complete the task."

"Oh, pardon me!" Mr. Leon protested. "Revolution is a serious matter, and not some prayer house burning. We sought to liberate the working masses from the capitalist grip. All evenhandedly, not just the Jews. Also Poles and Ukrainians. Because were things going so well for the Jews? That's right, was it a time of milk and honey for them? Roasted geese falling from the sky straight onto their plates? If things had been so good for them, they would not strive for the revolution, they would sit back and wait, like all the folks two hundred years ago, for the Lord to send them the Messiah. In our days!" he sneered.

"Within the life of the entire house of Israel, speedily and soon," finished Mr. Abram in earnest. "Do we believe in this at least a little?"

"Ve'imru omeyn," Mr. Chaim finished. "Liberate a Jew by knocking his hat off of his head. You all freed nothing." He showed Mr. Leon the fig sign.

"We haven't had the last word yet," Mr. Leon threatened, pointing his finger to Mr. Chaim.

"Better if you stop speaking. Enough."

Offended, Mr. Leon got quiet. Now, they were waiting for what Mr. Abram would say.

The latter waited for a moment until they stopped fidgeting.

"It had not begun with a revolution," he started slowly. "Don't you remember the history? Have you ever heard about assimilation?"

"About emancipation. That's what happened in Austria under His Majesty, Kaiser Franz Josef. And under the Prussian king. Equal rights. That Jews ought to be like other citizens. All equal under the law, no matter to which God you pray. The tsar was the only one to resist it." The Director decided to show off his knowledge.

"Haha! A load of baloney! The Prussian king came and liberated Jews. Austrian babble. Who did he liberate? Some bourgeoisie? Where did he get this?" Mr. Leon didn't try to hide his annoyance.

"Let him finish!"

Mr. Abram raised his hand and almost screamed at the wall: "Damned assimilation! Tell me, what Jew—a smart Jew, actually, even a dumb one, and plenty of dumb Jews come into this world—how can he believe in this idiotic notion that a Jew can swap the skin he's in and be somebody he's not?"

"Mr. Abram, admittedly, some managed," somebody observed.

"Managed? To become a goy? To dress up, go and dance to the tune he's given? Do you think it's so hard to convert?"

"Rubinstein, the pianist," Ms. Mala reminded.

"But Rubinstein, he's no apostate!" Ms. Tecia protested. "He only left the prayer house behind. Indisputably, he is a cultured man."

"Cut his nose," Mr. Leon laughed out loud. "That's what they said about this one guy who drank in a dive bar with the locals. Schicker vi a poyer, drunk like a peasant. Just that nose!"

"A nose was a sentence! There were too many nose experts," Mr. Chaim interjected acerbically. Mr. Leon sunk his head into his shoulders.

Mr. Abram continued.

"What, are there so many of us? What if each and every one converts?"

"That's all they want." Ms. Mala became invigorated. "Like back home in Vilnius before the war. Polish girls showed us and told us to kneel. And we kept running away in case someone would see . . . Holy Virgin who protects the bright city of Częstochowa and in a dark gateway passage you illuminate . . . See, I can still remember from public school," she rejoiced.

"A Jew should not go to church," Mr. Abram announced. "What for, what would you look for there? A bump on the head, surely."

"He's right on the money!"

"Mrs. Cukerman's daughter converted for her first husband,"

Ms. Mala reminded. "She was stupid and they pulled their hair out, worried over her, she even christened her child. But he left her anyway and fled with a shiksa," she added delightedly.

"So many years they've tried to get us on their side, but it never worked!"

"How many times did it work, it's impossible to count," Mr. Chaim pondered. "In Spain, where they burned Jews if they refused to spit on the Torah, in Ukraine, where the Cossacks wiped out thousands—children, women, old people. And the last time?"

"Hitler didn't care in the least if a Jew converted or not!" Mr. Leon called. "He wanted to . . . all of us," he stepped with his heel on a speck of dirt in front of him, "like that! Like bedbugs, like rubbish . . ."

"Yimakh shemo ve zikhro, obliterate his name and his memory," Mr. Abram chewed the curse in his mouth and spat.

"Thursday, prayers of atonement," the Director remembered. "Don't bring up his name, don't conjure up Hitler on a day before a holiday, Saturday is near."

"Hmm!" Mr. Leon pouted. "I'm beginning to like this."

Somehow everybody caught a chuckle. Only Mr. Chaim sat upset.

"Lately, I'm saying. Hitler is gone. Now they are changing Jewish holidays to different ones. Like an old coat for a new one. Supposedly it fits better. A better cut. And a carp tastes better in the winter than the Seder one in spring."

"That's what all the apostates repeated," Mr. Abram confirmed. "That a church is bright and a synagogue—dark and dirty."

"But do you really need to change your faith for this?" the Director shook his head. "To put new clothes on and go out to visit fancy houses. And chase the Lord out through the back door, for who needs him today? Just think about it, aren't we also guilty? Aren't we like a father who was so embarrassed to speak to his son in Yiddish that they never heard each other? Who throws holiday dinners for nonbelievers, and, on top of it, not our holidays, so that our close ones are turning in their graves looking at this."

"If they even have them." Mr. Chaim looked at him meaningfully.

"If they have them," the Director agreed. "If they even look at us, that nevertheless we've survived. But who are we now? And who were they?"

"They say one is a Jew if he has Jewish grandchildren," Mr. Abram banged the top of the table.

"It used to be, it used to be like this," Mr. Leon calmed him down.

Mr. Chaim was quiet for a moment. Easy for them to say. His son and daughter in Sweden. Grandchildren there. Not how it used to be, but at least something.

"And if he doesn't have any, if they were taken away from him, if they didn't want him to have them, who is he? A Jew? A goy? A freak of nature?" he asked unsurely.

"Then, he is a Jew from here. The only one of his kind," advertised the Director.

"Give it up," Ms. Mala requested. "A person tries to free herself from this."

"Thursday, prayers of atonement. The conversation came out like this," Mr. Abram gave a little smile.

He scratched his head.

"Thursday, a few hours, and the day is done. A long road before the Judgment Day. That's when those who are alive will be held accountable for their actions."

14

I WAS GETTING ready to leave when their bird-like voices rang around me again. The discreet cawing sounds of conversation. Like Mr. Leon and Mr. Abram back in the day behind a glass door. But it wasn't them. Like Doctor Kahn with . . . Also not. Somebody groaned and whined as if he were rolling enormous boulders. The shuffling of shoes. A familiar cough rumbled.

It's just the two of them: the Director and Mr. Jakub. They are still here, they haven't gone anywhere yet. The headman of the resort and his honorary guest, a resident of the last beit midrash on the first floor. His days are already numbered, but he's clinging to this world. He already knows that beyond extends the abyss of Sheol where he will never meet his Moshe Szpicer or his friends from the cheder on Nalewki 39. This is why he hangs around the other man, our host and master of ceremony, who every now and then adds to the Guest Register names of old guests—names nobody cares about. They bang about and wander the staircases from deep basements to attics, they drag their terrified bodies along the hallways and look for who knows what as if they wanted to catch rays of a sun that has already hidden behind the edge of the sky. This is their liturgy, their ardent, evening prayer, their praise to the Lord. It is their Blessed are You, Lord God, King of the universe, whose word calls forth the dusk of evening and whose wisdom opens gates. Before the arrival of the departed.

They paused across from me at the other end of the dining room. Two halves of a split shadow. Then, together we looked for a long time inside an empty common room where the dusk and an accompanying damp forest air were just descending on the library shelves full of books from Mr. Abram's and Ms. Tecia's collections.

A musty smell wafted through the room. The Director groaned under his breath.

"Riiiight . . ."

He seemed older than Mr. Jakub now. He looked around his kingdom. His tables and chairs, his broken ewer. For someone else's sins, not his, quite differently from what the prophet predicted.

He rested against the wall.

"We'll have to oil the hinges when spring comes, so they don't squeak," he mumbled.

"And you'll open the common room then?" the other one asked.

The Director turned his mouth down as if he'd just had a sip of a sour drink.

"Of course. We'll sit in the middle and play bridge," he laughed, "the two of us. We'll have peace and fresh air. Until the others find us. Holiday-makers," he sneeringly stressed the last word.

Mr. Jakub gave him a sign with his raised palm. No need to go too far. We always demand too much for ourselves. After all that happened, we still want life to come back here. Look at him. There are limits to chutzpah! Spring. A token reminder of our coming out of the house of bondage, which means a time of our freedom. April of that year, the one time that we were free. March, a few years later. You can continue to list. The whole calendar, eternity with a sentence sealed in the heavens even before a man's soul drops like a stone to earth.

"Holiday-Makers in the spring," he said loudly. "Don't worry, they won't arrive too soon. They're still young, what would they come here for? But wait a little, and you'll see."

The Director looked at him, surprised. What is he saying? An optimist on call. A friend to youth. An old fool! He hasn't gotten any smarter with age. Nearing his death, he began to believe in a bright future. Or maybe nobody got smarter? None of us, how many millions of us. Our empty place stands firm outside where at night the stars do not shine.

"The young will come," he drawled out. "Fine. Let them be, let them not go anywhere. They will stay, they won't be Jews, why would they be?"

Mr. Jakub wiped his half-closed eyes with his hand.

"The young ones will grow old, it is more than certain, and then they'll return to you." He was convinced of it.

"When they get old, not much will be left of them. Just the skin and bones, not counting worries," the Director observed.

Mr. Jakub shook his head with disapproval. A typical fool! What does he want? To take care of God's work, to turn back time and the order of things, to mix the evening with the dawn of a new day? Blessed be you, the Lord, who brings the dusk.

"Ani basar va dam, I am a man of flesh and blood," he recited slowly. "Isn't that what Moshe Rabbenu kept repeating to the Creator? Are we better than him? It is said: ninety-nine men depart this world due to worries, and only one because of God's sentence."

The Director chafed. He doesn't need to be explaining this! For each line in the Scripture, there are three in response. Our sages didn't hold back words in their teachings. Fat scrolls of parchment were filled from beginning to end, so that these two could have something to disagree over.

"How is this supposed to cheer me up if I won't live to see it?" he hissed with anger.

"Does a sage not plant a tree for the future generations?" Mr. Jakub asked in earnest. "Isn't that what Midrash tells us? A truth older than an immortal soul."

"Future generations poisoned," the Director lost his balance. "And the dust therefore shall be turned into pitch, which shall not be quenched night or day, and its smoke shall rise, and the earth, generation after generation, will be a desert. Upon which they will tread. Or, people like him, remnants."

He gave me a look. His eyes were burning. What are you still doing here? Stop snooping around, go back to your place, to your concerns, take to your heels and run fast, cut the ties. Forget and finally leave us alone.

"After we're gone, there won't be anything," he whispered.

Mr. Jakub refused to be provoked. He paced in place for a moment, looked at the Director with pity, and grunted, swallowing his anger:

"Here's a Jewish defiance! To spite yourself and me, you'll confuse Zion with Edom. To take away from others the last bits of hope! Where are they? Which they? What are you talking about?"

The Director was silent. Mr. Jakub went quiet. For a moment he massaged his high forehead and then spoke again, this time in a softer voice:

"Let him live. What does it bother you that he came here?"

He turned to me.

"Are you tired of us already? Right, young man? Better to go and catch girls than to listen to two old men."

The Director was mechanically fixing folded corners of an oilcloth tablecloth. He fished out of his pocket a wrinkly tissue and anxiously kept wiping away tea stains. Then he sat in his spot and hung his head sullenly.

"Jewish fate presses like a boulder." His head fell limply to the side. "They say, how blessed it is to be a Jew! You can almost collapse under this sweet weight," he laughed hysterically.

"He's lost it," Mr. Jakub declared. "Lost it completely!"

The other one pretended he didn't hear him. He just shivered, broken in half, cold, and his teeth chattering. Mr. Jakub covered him with his own wool sweater and when that didn't work, wrapped him in a printed tray-cloth brought from the lobby.

"I'll make tea later. Unless you want it . . ."

He bent over and whispered something in his ear. The headman of the boarding house shrank even more. Inside him something was rattling like trickling dry beans.

Mr. Jakub snorted impatiently. He looked my way and with his chin showed me out.

"It is time for us," he commanded. "Young man, do you have any luggage here?"

"Yes, I do, upstairs," I confirmed.

"In that case, we'll meet by the door in a minute. Go, get your stuff."

"Come on! No time to waste," he added, not really to himself or to the Director.

The latter did not move, visibly overwhelmed. He looked like a worn-out teddy bear, a rag doll from which crushed stuffing was escaping. He looked at Mr. Jakub with an expression of painful grievance.

"No need, stop! Why are you causing a scene?!" Mr. Jakub was visibly irritated. "You don't have to come with us, we'll go—just the two of us. You stay here. Better someone keeps an eye on the house," he put his hand on his shoulder.

The Director shrugged and whimpered,

"All alone?"

"I'll be back, I'll just walk him to the station."

"Fine, but don't take too long to get there." The Director suddenly regained his vigor and his need to grumble. "The evening is almost here. The forest is not safe now. You'll get lost on the way. What time is it? Will he still be able to catch a train?"

"Don't you worry, we'll manage," Mr. Jakub cut him off.

"Whatever you want. I'll be ready with dinner."

He walked into his office and shut the door behind him without saying goodbye.

Mr. Jakub looked at me impatiently. Let's go, finally.

Like our last walk with Mr. Leon in the Łazienki Park. Very old Mr. Leon. He was in prison with Grandpa once. His voice is failing him, so I can barely hear him, and only because Mr. Leon has told that story a hundred times or so, I can make sense of his fading words. At this moment, a squirrel jumps on our backrest and instantly climbs up on his shoulder as if Mr. Leon were already a piece of a dry stump that she can frolic upon with impunity. She sits there for a few seconds, and then, discouraged, she deftly jumps to the ground and dashes away. Our eyes follow her for a long moment until she disappears into tall grass. And there is no doubt—not a shred of it—that we will not meet again.

Mr. Jakub gave me a look to hurry up. Right, I'm coming. A gloomy lobby, worn-out seats with armrests, suburban train schedule hanging behind glass in a wooden display case, a corkboard with announcements. Exercise, physical rehabilitation, massages at home. The ugliness of the old wood paneling that I've just now noticed. Always squeaking stairs, two-tone walls, worn-out carpet mats. Nothing extraordinary, but they were drawn here. The mood. A tiny, dingy tabernacle in the desert, a place of rest during the journey. Our ark. Here, they were—we were—home. And we will always be here.

I slowly walked upstairs on tiptoe worried that any noisy movement might be inappropriate. Despite the care I took, my steps echoed in the hallway, bouncing dully from wall to wall. From afar I hear Doctor Kahn's sonorous laugh. Stay healthy, my companion! Here you don't get a minute's rest. In a moment, Ms. Hanka will visit him. Mr. Chaim's cough. With Mr. Abram, they will set up a game of chess on the terrace. Glasses. Mr. Abram got a bottle of cognac from his son in Sweden. A rhythmic tapping on the edge of the floor molding. That's from downstairs. Mr. Daniel is heading out for a walk. He and Grandma are talking about literature and about revolution. Mr. Daniel, too, was in prison with Grandpa. Now Grandma leads him by the hand. On the other side, Ms. Marysia, with a number underneath her gleefully flowered dress, is gleeful. Mr. Heniek with his dentures. Doctor Kaminska, the man without a hand. So many people, the same fate. That's what Mr. Leon used to say when he wanted to stop arguing with Mr. Abram. Our shared fate, but what do I care, who'd worry about fate, if in a moment we're taking a walk to the forester's lodge and I'll jump from pine tree to pine tree, certain that things will remain this way forever? Our shared fate. Mr. Abram agreed with Mr. Leon. What use is there in arguing? Doctor Kahn is laughing with his powerful voice. Somehow we'll live through it. What else can we do?

Here are the rooms of the first floor. One after the other. Each five steps by four, unless you get a suite. Doors wide-open. A rolled up rug by the armoire. A table, a cream-colored tablecloth, sheer cream curtains in the windows. On the bed, a neatly folded plaid blanket. A fluffed down pillow. Starched bedding, also folded, next to or on the blanket. A night table and a cone-shaped vase with a heather branch tucked into it. A basin, a tea glass in a metal holder, a plate, a spoon, a fork and knife. A shoe rack, a coat stand, and an umbrella holder. Ms. Tecia and Ms. Mala's rooms. And further down, the room that used to be ours. The same furniture, the same stuff. The same pressing silence of which I had a foretaste when everybody would lie down on beach chairs in the garden and motionlessly bask in the rays of a summer sun.

Familiar faces poked out from a stack of photos spread over the table. Here Uncle Szymon and Grandma wink at me, sending signals like a couple of students who skipped school and got caught on a romantic walk during a math class. As if they didn't freeze completely, as if they got stuck halfway between life and death. Trapped in a dance-like pose, and a fat man with a thick document folder, who before looked at Grandma covetously, follows them with his eyes, wanting to make sure they don't step beyond the edge of the frame since he can't make a move, glued to the sidewalk, with his head turned. And only his fedora slipped lower on his eyes, and his heavy overcoat, which strangely shows signs of age, like a wisp of smoke circling above a piece of hollowed-out, empty space.

I put them back in stacks. Grandmas, Uncle Szymons, Grandpa, cousins, and in-laws, family friends. Maybe the time has come to leave them here? The best place, they won't have a better one. When I am also gone, they—on paper prints—will become a bygone unknown crowd, a gathering of strange, blurry faces, like the ones in the portraits sold for pennies at flea markets. This way, they will lie in peace at the bottom of a drawer in one of the nightstands. I'll break its knob, so no one staying here later will feel like looking in there. Or better, I'll bury them in the ground, at the bottom of a ditch where Mr. Leon and I went on our dinosaur hunts that were supposed to bring us fame. Nobody will find them there, sand will cover them and softly wrap them in their sleep. I'll take them there.

Then I stood for a moment by the window staring at thinning

greenery. It was still light outside, and a warm sun spread like a cozy fold on the grass. Nearly leafless weed stalks revealed the not-so-distant view of the forest letting the sun bow slightly toward a glade overgrown with heather. A sharp, afternoon aroma of sand and warmed bark, wild herbs, and meadow flower swept into the boarding house, paying no attention to the domestic scents. The world was taking deep breaths, big swigs of resined air, and life in all its forms burst forth from everywhere, indifferent to switched-off chandeliers and dimmed wall lamps, as if it sought to take revenge on the old walls for their misery and infirmity and to swallow them completely, leaving behind them not even the tiniest tremble of memory.

15

MR. JAKUB WAITED on the veranda. He stood askew and poked about attentively with a stick in a garden planter. Over and over, he raised it to eye level and intently studied the consistency of the clods of clay stuck to the tip of the stick. He noticed me when I finally left the building, and he checked with respect my small backpack.

"Finally, sir, you made a decision, the last moment. I'd have left you here and walk to the train alone," he noted curtly.

Clearly, he was moved a little, ceremonial and embarrassed, and he tried to hide it under a mask of studied indifference.

"First, let's sit for a moment," he suggested. "You know, before hitting the road. It's an old Russian custom. Like drinking tea."

We set up two chairs facing the garden, like in a theater. Mr. Jakub comfortably stretched his leg. From a pocket of his overcoat he took out a few mint candies. He counted them in his palm and gave me half.

"It's sad to be among old people, isn't it?"

He didn't wait for my answer. "In any case, you were supposed to be here only for a few days . . . Passing by . . ."

Passing by. Youth is always in motion. That's what he probably wanted to add. Some passing by. A few days, a few moments, and I stayed my whole life. Indeed, it couldn't be any other way. I was brought here for my first vacation. And this house, this forest smelling of pinecones, their fate—I took part in it. I can't escape now.

"One more thing I wanted to tell you," he uttered hoarsely.

This means he's sick. Like his reb Szpicer. I won't see him again. One day, I'll come back here, or I won't, who knows what will happen, but one thing is certain, he won't be here, and I won't come across a friendly soul.

He turned to me. His eyes were blurry, the fire in his bulging eyes faded. I held my hand out to him.

"It is said that on the night when Jacob fell asleep in Beit El, the Lord let him see the entire history of the world. Just think about it: the entire history in one night! Isn't it too much for one man, even for the father of the twelve tribes? This is why, when he woke up, he only had strength to scream: What a terrible place! There is no doubt that God was here, and I knew nothing. *Va'ani lo yadati!*"

He spoke and I listened to his hoarse voice. It reached me from faraway, it didn't belong to the present day, it came from the unreachable depths of the past. I heard Mr. Jakub, maybe Doctor Kahn, and maybe even reb Moshe Szpicer as he was teaching the Midrash about the story of Jacob's wandering the pathless tracks of Canaan.

"And immediately, Jacob prayed and promised that if God walks with him, he too will walk with God. What type of agreement is this? How far can you go like this? Also, will the Lord always keep his promise?"

He grew upset.

"Abraham went into the unknown, because that's what God told him to do. Lekh lekha meartzecho. Get thee out of thy country, umimoladtecho. From thy kindred. And then it says from thy Father's house. So Jacob left his home to come back as Israel. And we? Each year we go out of Egypt, on Pesach, you know this, sir. And each year we go back. And where is this Promised Land?"

Impatiently, I shifted my feet. Just to make sure he doesn't catch me. And then, my whole time here, day, night, and day again, stood before my eyes together with all the previous days in this place. Or maybe I just thought I saw them in the diminishing eyes of the other man?

"Abraham didn't resist the Eternal. The Lord told him, so

he went, not asking what for, or why. And Jacob? He actually fought. We, Jews, always try to argue with the Lord, even if we doubt his existence. We have stiff necks and hard backs, but he, up there, der eybershteyr, ribono shel oylam, responds harshly. Many blows of the cane he delivered upon us for our sins. Our skin is hardened, so hard you can write on it the words of our holy Torah."

A ball of ripe sun began to descend behind the crowns of the tallest pine trees. It got chilly. An early evening's damp air quickly filled the forest.

"Ready?" he livened up and gave a sign to go.

He's not doing so badly, there'll be many others he'll walk with. We walked across the lawn passing a bed of begonias, a few benches and a gate, and walked onto a forked gravel road. The shape of our building was becoming blurry and disappearing behind the first pine trees, as if it were a forest hut, or a dog-house, tiny and unworthy of remembering. Early on, between the tree trunks its details were popping up: lean pillars of the dining room, tall windows of the ballroom, slender chimneys, upper windowpanes . . . but they too were quickly disappearing behind oncoming trees, which in turn, were rapidly turning into shadows. And before I even noticed, the boarding house disappeared completely.

We were only a few steps away from the station, the train was supposed to come soon, when Mr. Jakub paused. I was sure he wanted to say goodbye, yet he spoke in a voice that would allow no dissent.

"Let's go, there is still time. Let me show you something."

He led. We made a circle, leaving behind us the edge of the concrete platform covered with a lush blackberry bush. And we marched ahead—on a wide, sandy road that soon turned into a narrow sand alley that led deep into the forest where heavy oaks now bowed to the ground with their mass of reddening leaves. We walked fast in the thicket and grass lit up with a layer of autumn gold, just like the first time I came here. We took turns, walked back and forth, getting lost in the forest to the rhythm of Mr. Jakub's silent steps. We walked long enough that my legs began to hurt. Mr. Jakub marched with determination, in his overcoat and with nothing on his head, an old head like the globe Mr. Leon showed me in the photos taken from the moon.

He actually reminded me of Mr. Leon, it seemed like it was his shoulder nudging me just in case, as if he could not believe that I was still walking with him here. He walked stepping on pinecones, and they cracked under the soles of his worn-out shoes. He led me deep into the forest where I'd never been before. He looked like a forest monster—he creaked, wheezed, and crunched. He was in a terrible hurry, trying to get ahead of his weakening breath, he rushed against his tired lungs. He deftly jumped over pits, evaded junipers and beds of ferns; with a stick he drew back pine branches and caught the last cobwebs of gossamer that flew over his face.

At times, he paused for a fraction of a moment, and focused as he searched for the right direction, and then he waded into an even deeper thicket, briskly cutting through bushes of thistle or raspberries that were getting stuck to his overcoat, sticking to his wool pants, not wanting to let him go further. He got ahead and only his birdlike skull appeared above the thick greenery. It swam alone as if on waves, detached from a tiny body hidden by leaves of blueberries, a body that probably also steadily pushed ahead, aware of the quickly approaching dusk. He didn't pay attention to me anymore, I didn't matter to him. It was obvious that he wanted to continue the journey alone. However, I didn't have the courage to leave him alone in the middle of a forest, and I was also probably worried that without his help I wouldn't know my way back. Willy-nilly, I followed him, I let him lead me into the wilderness where we would both get lost and where we would have nothing else to do but to wander aimlessly through eternity.

Finally, the forest gave way, slightly. We walked along the weedy and slippery edge of a lake, and squeezing through one or two groves, we continued on our path. It seemed now like we were walking toward the end of this world and that we would continue to walk, tripping again and again over roots of pine trees that resembled Mr. Abram's gnarled palms and blindly grasping stinging nettles and other flimsy weeds until we fell to the ground or until we took a shortcut and like moles we started digging tunnels in the sinking ground. Then we climbed up a steep dune, our steps quickly vanishing behind us in the sand. Each needle trembled in the wind, almost translucent as the last rays of sun penetrated through it. Each branch of heather bent its back under Mr. Jakub's firm steps as if he were a ruler of the surrounding nature and not an old man from a boarding house who had gone out for an evening walk.

When we reached the top of a small hill, and the fog again lay in thick billows, Mr. Jakub looked at the bushes nearby and then finally stopped. He whispered something under his breath for a while, he had a mysterious conversation with himself, then he struck his stick against the ground—he swung so hard that a cloud of dust rose above the forest undergrowth. And suddenly the place swarmed with the boarding house residents—like in the old days in our garden. They were older than before but more familiar in their dark overcoats, plaid jackets, and collars of real fur, in their hats and side caps, Oxford shoes and moccasins that made it easier for me to recognize who was who.

Doctor Lewin was there, advertising the advantages of the boarding house, and his assistant, Doctor Centnerszwer, and Aunt Grunia and cousin Abrasza, Ms. Tecia's sister, and Moses—the one who went to fight in the war in Spain, Świętojerska 11, annex in the courtyard, second floor with a view on the yard, and his brother Israel, who was then listed in the book of Izaak Feldwurm, next Attorney Kirszenberg from Bat Yam, Professor Wolpe, Doctor Kahn's doppelgänger with a roll of paper, Mr. Lifszyc in a hat of white linen, the Rabinowicz family, Pesja, Gienia's mother and merchant Lewi, Ms. Regia's father, a fashion magazine, an address on a business card, Grandma and Grandpa, people from the boarding house and the ones from Aleja Przyjaciół—Friendship Avenue, who never came to visit us in the boarding house, people from here and from there, whom I knew only from laminated postcards with beautiful stamps, those who are alive and those who passed away long ago. And the ones who walked out, and those—and that was the majority, who could have walked out with them but stayed. And the ones who escaped but for nothing. And others who walked out of Egypt facing destruction and whom the Almighty lost on the way so that not the slightest trace of them was left.

"Just don't tell anyone!" Mr. Jakub grabbed me and clutched me so hard that my bones cracked and dark spots on his hands suddenly got darker, almost turning black, like a dead man's.

"Oh, dear God!" he moaned in Mr. Leon's voice. I looked at him, surprised because until now Mr. Leon never dared to utter God's name.

Then I only heard single, clipped words.

"And then, there were six hundred thousand of us, that's what is said. Why did you lead us out of the house of bondage? Would it not be enough for you to keep us there but alive? Would we not be happier without your Torah?"

The crowd in overcoats made a sound. What is he thinking? He lost his mind, finally, he went crazy and that's that! But nobody intended to answer him, and he continued speaking with great devoutness:

"Dear God, better break this chain of crippled generations already! Break and stop, take me and the others back with you. Take us under the wings of your presence and comfort us there, so we can fall asleep in peace and happiness and so that nightmares won't come to us. And let us be bound in the bond of life."

"Amen!" the boarding house residents finished. By now it was impossible to tell them apart from the surrounding junipers. He now ran around like a madman, shaking the tip of his stick.

I wanted to escape but I felt that something was holding me, chaining me to this place, and not letting me move, as if my legs were roped, as if I belonged to the generation of Mr. Abram and Ms. Mala, as if there was no age difference between me and Uncle Szymon, not even the tiniest crack to separate our fates from each other. They held me in a steel embrace.

"I'm coming to you!" I shouted.

"Nah, where did you get this idea? Crazy, he simply went crazy! What kind of silly things is he saying?"

"It is our forest and we don't need anyone else!"

"He's Bronka's grandson. Where will he go now?"

"Where was he then? Maybe he wasn't there at all?"

The last from a chain of generations, clutching at the very end.

It was late into the night when I reached the station.

Piotr Pazinski was born in Warsaw in 1973. He is the author of two books on James Joyce. His debut novel, *The Boarding House*, won the European Union Prize for Literature in 2012.

Tusia Dabrowska teaches at SPS New York University and at the Uniwersytet Warszawski. She was part of a documentary by Adam Zucker entitled *The Return: A Documentary about Being Young and Jewish in Poland.*

CPSIA information can be obtained
at www.ICGtesting.com
Printed in the USA
BVHW070922301218
536649BV00006B/7/P

9 781628 972726